CHRISTOPHER

GRIMES

THE

PORNOGRAPHERS

The Pornographers

a novel by
Christopher Grimes

Jaded Ibis Press
sustainable literature by digital means™
an imprint of Jaded Ibis Productions U.S.A.

© 2012 copyright Christopher Grimes

Second edition. All rights reserved.

ISBN: ISBN-13: 978-1-937543-20-4

Library of Congress Control Number: 2011937988

Printed in the United States of America. No part of this book may be used or reproduced in any manner whatsoever without written permission from the publisher, except in the case of brief quotations embodied in critical articles and reviews. For information please email: questions@jadedibisproductions.com

Published by Jaded Ibis Press, *sustainable literature by digital means*™ An imprint of Jaded Ibis Productions, LLC, Seattle, WA USA jadedibisproductions.com

Cover art by Scott Zieher. Cover design by Debra Di Blasi.

This book is also available in full color, ebook and fine art limited editions. Visit our website for more information.

Excerpts from this manuscript have appeared in *Beloit Fiction Journal* and *KNOCK*.

for Maria Luisa Basualdo
without whom this book would not have been written

WINTER 2001
The United States of America

The next to last item before the Budget Committee, a proposal for a direct-to-Internet video production — tentatively titled *Flight 69* and told, we're briefed, exclusively through the eyes of the main character (evidently some dude named Abdul) — finds us airborne in an aisle seat, the black and white countdown leader of an in-flight movie flickering at the front of the cabin, next to which, the movie screen, stands a severe-looking flight attendant, described as one of those stone-faced Frigidaires all buttoned up with her hair pulled back, her mouth a glossy, thin-lipped scar, none of which strike us as too promising, what with the antiseptic and generally problematical setting of an airplane, to say nothing of all the scowling, until it's revealed that the in-flight movie is actually an adult feature, a solemn orgy filmed and presented in vintage Super 8, a welcome development despite its contributing to an already overly-complicated scenario, including, it's pointed out, such additional logic discrepancies as

to how the feature was pre-loaded into the inter-
cabin entertainment system in the first place (one
wonders aloud if we have the makings of a comedy
here), but even these more or less logistical
concerns now evaporate, at least temporarily,
with the revelation of the extraordinarily sexy
specimen we're introduced to, sitting right next to
us in the window seat, a stone-cold knockout
squeezing out dollops of hand cream on her hands,
rubbing the hand cream in, dollopful by dollopful,
periodically glancing at us, languidly pushing an
auburn curtain of hair aside with the top of her
oily wrist so that we can see the blunt, rounded
tops of her teeth and a suggestion of the tongue
there in the pink center of a seductive, full lipped
smile, prompting us to speak, to ask (importantly,
it's emphasized) *to where is* [*sic*] *you going*, delivered
almost in a whisper, the effect defined as some
kind of foreign accent, one she's perhaps having
difficulty placing, too, because she's still just
sitting here mutely, still just smiling, continuing

to rub that hand cream on her hands, probably wondering, as we do, if the accent is along the lines of an Arnold Schwarzenegger, say, who sounds a lot to us like a younger Henry Kissinger, when she finally offers up her singular reply, drawing out the word *vacation*, snapping the lid of her hand cream shut after saying it, our gaze moving jerkily from the hand cream bottle to her breasts — described here as not too big and not too little, definitely natural, just *right* — although it's imperative to the plot, we're told, that we peel our eyes off of them, what's described as that stupendous rack of hers, and instead look back down to the tray table that's been obscuring a view to our lap, lifted now to reveal that in our one hand is a gun, and in the other, an enormous erection, an erection so impressive in its enormity that Hot Babe drops her hand cream, a look of horror on her face (we don't know if it's the gun or the erection pointed in her direction that frightens her at this point), a look on her face that clearly

comprehends the instant truth of the matter that
we ourselves give voice to — that *this shit going* [*sic*]
down, bitch, and so are you — and after giving it, the
harrowing pronouncement, we reach out and grab
her by the arm, forcing her to stand up for the
purpose of dragging her to the front of the aircraft,
right up to where the severe looking, buttoned-up
Frigidaire stands, presumably still at the spot
where earlier she had demonstrated the adjustment
mechanism of our seat belts, and where she
continues to stand, a force to be reckoned with,
because we're taking control of this plane,
goddamnit, taking over Flight 69, and in clear
demonstration of the fact, we briskly shove
Frigidaire out of the aisle, pluck the inter-cabin
telecom unit off the wall and announce that *you
American bitches, exporting your lust and various so-
called degradations and seductive ways* — something
along these lines, it's explained, as this is simply a
rough sketch and some dialogue will need to be
re-, well, thunk — *well, now you will see what it*

means to get fucked, we command, motioning to suddenly not-so-severe-looking, but still humorless Fridge (her flight attendant cap having fallen off from the shove, she now stands to reveal a glowing mane of blonde hair) with the barrel of our gun, and we order her, the once frigid figure now thawing before our eyes (things are getting a bit complicated, it's admitted), to *come here*, an order that she at once obeys (we maintain both gun and erection, after all), nervously stepping toward us, taking tentative, sideways looks at the passengers, her charges, as if to spy the answer to the question of why, exactly, she's here in the first place, what her purpose is, what she should do next, a studied and severe authority (albeit increasingly sexy), fortuitously conversant in and therefore presumably able to translate the incomprensible language we're barking at our captive audience (in other words, we appear to have exhausted our English vocabulary by this time in the presentation), which she does, translate, for the rest of the passengers, all of whom we are surprised to now discover are women, who must, the flight attendant says on our behalf, take off their pants and skirts, and now their shirts, followed by the bra and those panties, so that when everyone is sitting in their seats naked, we pick Hot Babe up — the other, initial passenger, not the hot, at this point, Flight Attendant — and turn her over in mid-air, her legs pointing straight up like fireplace tongs, which we proceed to spread, the legs/ tongs, and run our tongue along the folds of her vagina, momentarily stopping to tell Flight Attendant to tell her, Hot Babe whose vagina we're licking, to reciprocate (for such is the Flight Attendant's dilemma, the contract that she has with Hot Babe, and indeed all the other passengers, that she must faithfully deliver our demands in order to save them all, an unenviable position, to be sure, and one that we doubtless relate to), executed, the fellatio, at first hesitantly and in great fear, and *voila*, a standing 69 — hence the

title — although thusly engaged we still frequently eye the other passengers suspiciously, we're told, but they, too, are getting aroused (in any event our point of view reveals that there's lots of lip licking among them), so we wave the gun, telling now naked Flight Attendants to communicate our directive that *you American sluts, you get fucking or else*, and that's all it takes, apparently, because there's a sudden swarm of groping, a *fuckfest,* someone offers, *at 30,000 feet,* citing the description as possible promotional copy, which, particularly as we're beginning to run short on time — to say nothing of the fact that the decision of whether or not we really want to pursue actual production, as opposed to just the distribution of content is still a source of serious debate — provides an opportune segue to the other, related item on the agenda, *Trends Analysis*, though before leaving the first item for the moment, it should be made clear that despite the obvious cost prohibitions of the scenario just reviewed (re:

setting, specifically the building or procuring of a
commercial aircraft hull), it represents the kind of
out-of-the box thinking that might well get us
through our critical, at this point critically *chronic*
budget shortfall, and although we're given to
understand that this was a summary of part one of
the entire production, and part one only, we agree
it's sufficiently illustrative of the general thrust of
the concept, and that, despite the obvious financial
restrictions such a production would be made to
labor under, it deserves further consideration
(though perhaps in a modified form), but be that as
it may, for the moment at least, we'd do well to
put it aside in order to get to the second item on
the agenda, the Comptroller's analysis of trends,
rooted, he prefaces, squarely in the Pew Charitable
Trust's latest poll indicating that a full 82.5% of
American males aged 18 to 40 accessed Internet
pornography at least once last month, that 33.6%
of American females in the same age group are
reported to have accessed Internet pornography

during the same period, both trajectories therefore leading us to the inescapable conclusion that there's lots and lots and lots of accessing of pornography *via* Internet going on even as he, the Comptroller, speaks, that the accessing of Internet pornography has become a mainstream, so-called populist activity, statistically speaking (although, he says, given the relatively narrow scope of the Pew study, certain extrapolations needed to be made to account for broader demographics, and that we therefore might need to adjust our business plan accordingly in order to accommodate such information, as encouraging as it is), a statistical spike in consumer demand perhaps on the one hand attributable to — and here the Comptroller is just thinking out loud — the sudden, widespread availability of low cost, high quality digital cameras allowing a producer to focus on creating output that appeals to the more idiosyncratic and fetishistic tastes of the consumer, tastes historically too narrow in their interests for a producer with

mass-market ambitions, and, on the other, all of
the demands, simply speaking, made on our time,
the fact that we have no more time *left*, the
Comptroller continues, not a spare minute, plain
and simple, nothing more than a couple of minutes
maybe to do *anything*, so that the average, basic
consumer isn't going to waste his time with all the
rigmarole that gets in the way of the excitement,
no, because he *needs* the thing right here, right
now, and besides pornography is pretty much your
Reader's Digest condensed version anyway — what
with its short build up, etcetera, as per discussion
in the earlier example — all boiling down to
expectation, because that guy who's thinking
about the quote, unquote cum shot (a theme that
he'll take up more diligently later in his analysis,
he says) is thinking about the so-called cum shot
long before he sits down in front of the computer,
meaning this guy's on the bus thinking about that
cum shot, reading the lists of names of the dearly
departed in the newspaper obits while vaguely

thinking about that cum shot waiting at home for him, so that when he *does* finally get there (home), he kisses the wife and children, finds himself a little privacy in the basement down there next to the washer and dryer, monkeys around for thirty seconds (the word is surfs, someone suggests) until he finds the thing he's after, then afterwards goes upstairs and throws a few lawn darts with the kids before dinner and life goes on, the point being that it's the way things are heading, and the problem is going to be trying to keep a market share against all the competition for viewership — never minding for the moment those couple of Arabs, to give just one instance, who sure as hell knew what they're doing with regard to making a spectacle of themselves — competition here specifically referring to the deep and trenchant issues involved in just how one is supposed to compete for time and attention, basic problems created by some pretty cut-throat forces whose only goal is to suppress their competitors' product

identity, but anyway, the Comptroller says, if we
turn to Agenda Item II, of the analysis of trends,
we arrive at the cliché that there's nothing new
under the sun, because as successful pornography
is made into something always already known by
the general consuming public, the report before
us indicates specialized productions tend to
disappear from view, a fact supportable by some
impressively persuasive graphs and charts if our
Power Point projection unit wasn't still on the
fritz, forcing us to forgo the glitz and glam, we're
told, and instead we'll get straight to the bottom
line here, which is that the big draw today is still
oral sex with female as the giver and male as
receiver, and that we're to continue to view the
so-called cum shot, also known as the *money shot*
for good reason, as a mandatory sign of sexual
climax, a compulsory indication that pleasure is
achieved, a marketing sign, furthermore, fully
born out by the research, firmly indicating that
what's true on VHS tape in the 1980s and 90s

holds true in today's online environments, perhaps even more so, suggesting perhaps increased investment in the money shot, especially if resources are limited, as they so desperately are, so that we might as well forget everything else in this analysis, we're told, and simply *let it all ride* on the money shot — the Comptroller's just kidding a little here, he confesses — which nevertheless brings him to a tertiary point involving promotion, including such findings that of figures presented in advertising our adult website, it's recommended that a full 72% be female, specifically, in terms of descriptor and frequency of descriptor historically employed, *thin* (98%), *young* (92%) and *white* (66%), with *long* (84%) and *blonde* (48%) hair, while male figures should almost exclusively be present only as phallus, with the rest of the male body being framed out, especially the head and face, thus affecting a kind of anonymity and omnipresence at the same time, an unidentifiable but imperative presence, it's emphasized, critical

even (or especially) to the success of those cases
marketed as *lesbian*, wherein the reproduction of
girl-on-girl action must crucially include the
possibility of the male consumer to join in, as
implied by the lesbians performing fellatio on
polymer penis-like-objects, for instance, while
gazing toward the camera, the act suggesting the
penis, or penis-like-object, as the assumed source
of pleasure in lesbian sex while reminding the
voyeur of the power of his own peanut, itself
described in terms of descriptor and frequency in
promotional material as *big* (45%), *monster* (17%),
huge (12%), *over 12 inches* (9%), *fat*, or its synonym
thick (8%) and *massive* (4%), depending on
advertising budget (virtually none), in contrast to
the descriptors historically used for female
genitalia — *tight* (73%), *tiny* (11%), *little* (8%) and
small (8%) — as it, the female genitalia, acts for all
intents and purposes as the point of entry into the
milieu itself, the story, its simplicity, we're told,
really impossible to overemphasize, inasmuch as

research reveals that it is as it has always been in mainstream culture, meaning that arousal is best achieved through the use of stock characters, since complex and contradictory characters evoking complex emotions tend to decrease and disturb the experience (translation: once the scene is set, we can get down to the *real* action) though word to the wise, we're warned, while templates produce a certain degree of repetition and familiarity, they do not dictate the content or meaning of the experience in question, speaking of which, before we adjourn, if there aren't any at this point, meaning questions, this might be a good time to reiterate that we've already established a long and documented history of being open to creative revenue sources such as these — we'd do well to think here of *Bob Lerner's Field Guide to Animal Tracking in the American Midwest* just published by our own DNR, as well as the grant matching for the Variable Road Surface Study from mile markers 264 through 282 on the Fieldings Expressway, to

cite just two recent examples — entitling this
Committee to assert with some degree of certainty
that our possible foray into online adult
entertainment will finally be seen as about as
exciting and controversial as watching someone
reading the tax code, discussing investment
portfolios, singing the merits of long versus short
term liquidity, droning on about turn-over rates
and capital trends, all delivered in coffee breath
and forced by bloat (plus we simply can't afford to
take anything off the table at this point), and that
therefore we should continue to forge ahead in this
direction, speculatively speaking, of course, all
the while being cognizant of such pertinent little
legal dramas like the one unfolding over there in
Salt Lake City, furthering our investigation, for
instance, in such germane matters as just what it
means to be *obscene*, the term itself, as defined by
the statute coming down from the Fed to the State
to us, stipulating that the material is definitionally
obscene if it's found offensive to the *average* person,

applying contemporary community standards espoused by the average citizen of Salt Lake City in this case, to whom the vendor in question is averaging four thousand adult video sales a month, a fraction of the adult entertainment consumed by the average citizen of Salt Lake, who is reportedly acquiring five times that amount through cable, satellite and Internet sources, as verified by our Comptroller in the conclusion of his written report, itself containing some intriguingly promising statistics, not the least of which is the fact that a full 50 percent of those staying in hotel rooms offering pay-per-view purchase a so-called adult feature, contributing to a $10 billion dollar annual industry in the United States alone, with a potential for a 377% profit margin (that's 377%, not 3.77% or 37.7%), all of it transacted aboveboard and out in the open, not in some sleaze ball operation with a store front in a strip mall (not that there's anything wrong with strip malls, per se), we mean blue chip parent companies

— General Motors, AT&T — multi-nationals
headed by the likes of Mitt Romney and Rupert
Murdoch, not some guy in Reno who's asking us
to fork over a couple hundred thousand, hoping he
doesn't disappear into the desert in a rusted El
Camino, to say nothing of the fact that most
municipalities are *already* invested in various forms
of adult entertainment, as in the tinny environs of
AT&T stock, for example, where beats the lusty
heart of their Hot Network, or take DirecTV,
through which GM sells more sexually explicit
material than Larry Flynt ever dreamed of, to say
nothing   of   Hilton,   Comcast,   Marriott
International, so give us a break, we'll say to the
skeptics, we're already *in* the business of such
service providing that, even as we speak, is moving
away from its traditional base, the weary traveler
on an overnight layover between Boise and Boston
who desires to partake of a little more provocative
viewing than a bodice ripper on the *Late-Late Show*,
who instead can now access such entertainment

piped, as it were, directly into the privacy of one's home, as the citizens of Salt Lake can attest (they have already spoken clearly on the matter), affording us the opportunity to state with unanimous certainty that the future of adult entertainment is indeed online, an eminently supportable prediction that, now arrived upon (incidentally, good work, people), concludes another formal inquiry and subsequent presentation of recommendations happening daily in municipal government, the seemingly mundane, accruing progression of decision-making our average citizen hopes to remain happily unaware, an endless procession of what appear to be minor choices made that directly contribute to the greater good, as exemplified, to foreshadow an immediate matter at hand, by the strict ordinances on signage up for renewal tomorrow morning, and how this one decision alone results in keeping up certain appearances that, although visitors and even locals are hard pressed to put a finger on it, everyone calls *nice*, because therein lies the effect (the secret's no neon, of course), constituting yet another perfect illustration of how facts determine facts in the municipal mesh, how, to give another example, the linear, causal logic of our building codes prohibits the erection of structures more than four stories high because the soil is so rich and loamy, not at all suited for bearing the stress and footprint of tall building, thus ensuring that everything's therefore built to moderate scale, resulting in the appearance of our homes looking genuinely homey, instilling in us the credo that modesty is our policy (bring the kids, stay for the day, stay for the rest of your lives), giving weight to the proposal of our new slogan — *You're Welcome* — all of which should remind us, at moments such as these, how little we lacked in the old days, and how time changes every single thing, such that one moment it's business as usual, and the next, *The Price Is Right* is preempted by the now familiar images of the World Trade Center on fire, the

images of the airplanes penetrating the towers, the repeating shots of fiery jet fuel spraying out of them, and how, one directly after another, it seems, they collapse, imploding, tumbling down onto themselves into a massive cloud of dust, and when that, too, is spent, what's left but the ideal space that was there before their erection, an unbelievable emptiness that makes us yawn at the sight of it, as if the truth of the images is just too exhausting to take in all at once, until one telephone rings, and then another, and suddenly the whole phone bank, seemingly every phone on every floor of the entire Municipal Hall is ringing all at once in the noisy, chaotic beginning of such a terrible day, as everybody now knows, that seems to simply repeat itself, the bombing in the morning, and now, as if it were the afternoon of the very same day, our continued, seemingly unending deliberations on calamity mitigation, the costs thereof, what with Hazmat suits at $550 per, not including breathing apparatus, not including boots, not including disaster control or the appropriate vehicles to get on-scene in a manner befitting, or take the purchase and replacement costs of those detonation robots, which don't come cheap (and yet when a suspicious something needs blowing up per newly mandated regulation, we can't simply go out and borrow one), nor, for that matter, can we afford to sit idly by and continue ogling the option packages available for that Kenworth thirty-two foot T300 Mobile Control and Command Center equipped with limited slip-locking differential brakes, Jacobs Extarder, 5-speed automatic transmission, one touch electric awning, street side workstations, overhead storage cabinets, hinged dry erase locking boards, removable task swivel chairs, drop-in insertable conference table, bulkhead divider with sliding doors, Kenmore microwave, Sanyo refrigerator, Black & Decker 12 Cup Spacemaker Coffee Maker, four thirty-two inch Sharp LCD TVs, a Sony DVD/VCR player,

Hughes receiver, HP All-In-One color printer,
Ratheon IR-360 Dual Camera (including thermal
and night vision systems), Shurflo Extreme 5.7
gallons per minute water pump, 30 gallon fresh
and gray water tanks, Kenwood Marine speakers,
Phone Patch Block EVI, Tellular Phone Cell Fixed
Wireless Terminal, Orion All-In-One Weather
Station, dual battery selector switch, 120/240
Marathon Diesel power generator, Moto-Sat 1.2
meter Internet satellite and KVH Trac Vision #S3
Mobile Digital Satellite dishes, all tricked out in
neon green, preferably, to match the other vehicles
in our Emergency Management fleet, because we
need one, because we have to start thinking of our
own and play the hand we're dealt, a hand we
should make no apologies for playing, so while the
Rotarian faction in particular will want it to be on
record that we hadn't been going around looking
for capital investments in on-line adult
entertainment, when the idea presented itself we
can say we took it up, our hand (we are in need of

so many things) just as it was dealt, without
flinching at the cards, our gaze and hands steady,
our cards on the table for everyone to see (indeed,
our community leadership strives for such
transparency as this), all under the watchful eye of
Public Relations, who is advising full disclosure
— here's a headline, *Mayor stands firm* [in his
conviction that he continues to speak the interests
of the people] — so if some potato spud from the
Shopper, or anywhere else for that matter, thinks
there's a scoop here, there's not, unless one can
call the endless compromises that lie before us a
scoop, then by all means stop the presses and bring
the cameras to this afternoon's scheduled
negotiations between the Mayor himself (who's
late for a Citizen Counsel meeting and has to
scoot, but will, he says, catch up with us at the HR
brownbag), our Director of Parks and Recreation,
and the Women's Auxiliary for Peace (WAP),
formerly WYC (Women's Yoga Club), who,
already ruffled by rumors that their trip to India

will be indefinitely postponed because of increased
travel restrictions (the rumors are true), will
undoubtedly come to the meeting on the defensive
in their latest attempt to lobby for the carpet to be
removed at the Stillman Recreation Facility, the
rug removed and replaced with a so-called floating
laminate flooring more conducive to their club's
activities — the organizing principle of their
former incarnation, the yoga, now deployed as the
primary weapon, they say, in the enforcement of
their self-described peace keeping mission (yawn)
— and, if that weren't enough, they're also
requesting the installation of a series of wall
mounts from which ropes can be hung, apparently
for the purpose of hanging themselves, the
members of WAP, upside-down, an expenditure
that has no chance of approval, believe us, and
besides, we feel we've already been more than
materially supportive of their activities, seeing
that their Wednesday Night WYC, initially started
shortly after the September 11 catastrophe,

became a Tuesday and Thursday night affair, soon giving way to a Monday, Wednesday, Friday schedule, and has now become a standing reservation for an 8am and 6pm class, Monday through Saturday, with a Sunday Yoga Brunch starting at 11am, when twenty or thirty women lie spread across the floor, trying to mimic corpses in the late morning light, the scene a little spooky, a little macabre, frankly, as is their deep and raspy breathing when they're doing it, trying to become corpses, while their teacher, the principal of the middle school, their representative to this afternoon's negotiations — that elfish, big haired pain in the ass shaped, as she is, uncannily like a human thumbtack — waxes on about such things as the space between thoughts, reprieves and respites — what's the phrase, *a period of thoughtless repose* (just stick it in a Hallmark card, sister) — forcing us to come to negotiations a little more literal-minded, as in we'll be going in armed with a pediatric defibrillator, not the defibrillator per se

(this is exactly the point), but the pediatric defibrillator's promotional material, including mechanical sketches sent to us by the company manufacturing them, so that on the one hand we'll have WAP's proposed work order, and on the other, the requisition form for the defibrillator, along with the six-inch stack of unfilled requests for the emergency management equipment we're so desperately in need of, our intention being to overwhelm her with the facts on reams and reams and reams of paper, affording us the opportunity to instead put the choice to her, the Thumbtack, after pointing to the stack of papers (the elephant in the room) and informing her that these are the appropriation recommendations from the Federal Government, what they say we need for disaster mitigation in the event of another terrorist attack, which the Federal Government says is imminent, creating the present fiscal dilemma to either blow our wad on her floor, we'll say, or, alternatively, we can buy us this little incidental (here we open the defibrillator brochure purposefully topping the stack), because it's a simple matter of biological fact that we can't use an adult defibrillator on a child, it'll kill the kid, never minding for the moment that most of the classified neurotoxins are designed to do just that, inhibit respiration, inasmuch as if you're a kid and you've been exposed to a neurotoxin, you're going to need a pediatric defibrillator, so go ahead and make a choice here, the poor kid's mother is waiting, and take your sweet time while we sit back and eyeball this invoice for an unbelievably expensive portable atmospheric synthesis unit — we mean *relax*, but *choose* — because, believe us, ever since the attack on these United States of America, we too have noticed that things are getting a little tense on the home front, what with the attack itself, which is brutal enough, but add to that staffing shortages in the Information and Technologies Department, the inability to find a comfortable sleeping position in the last trimester, one count of embezzlement,

asbestos found in the old Brach's Candy factory condo development, lost retainers at $225 a pop, health insurance policies denying coverage for physical therapy, catastrophic budget deficits at the municipal, State and Federal levels (of course), another mild stroke in the ranks, threats of celibacy, the odd melanoma, life, which, believe us, can't be forgotten with just one night at Jacuzzi Suites, as nice of a night as it might have been, so take your time, we'll say, *choose*, thereby ensnaring her in the brute logic of the dilemma, compelling her (hopefully) to see just how pitifully mundane WAP's yoga floor problem is compared to the responsibilities we daily shoulder for the community entire, and while we're at it, we might as well go ahead and emphasize our absolute prohibition on air travel, conducted in accordance with recommendations made by our own State Department, so that therefore their trip to India is indefinitely canceled, the news of which will undoubtedly be met by a majority of the women with some hostility, especially, they'll argue, since their plans for air travel have been some many months in the making (well, that's just too bad), requiring our reaffirmation here that our position will not change — our position is no air travel under *any* circumstances — regardless the inevitability that the majority of the women's position is that we shut up and shove our position, a response so predictable in fact that we are fully prepared to confront what we've come to term the Indian Impasse, come to us by way of the general relationship advice we've been compiling in earnest in order to build our rebuttal, amounting to an attempt at an all-out diffusion of the hostile delivery of their position by pointing out its hostile phrasing, how it needs to be said now that inasmuch as shutting up doesn't really provide a neutral blank for its intended receiver to fill, not really, we should agree to just go ahead and skip that sort of thing, the telling of someone to shut up, because if we've learned anything lately, we'll point out,

we should have learned to be a little nicer to each other, because if all it took was shutting up, that'd be easy, wouldn't it, though, predictably, the women's position will remain that the problem is not when to shut up, but, egregiously (for all parties involved), not being able to *make* someone shut up, not now, not here, not *ever*, all delivered with the conviction of a professional diagnosis when, as a point of fact, there's probably not one among them qualified to give such a diagnosis, probably not, so what it *actually* amounts to, we'll say, is yet another personal opinion, in the same vein as, for example, an earlier, so-called professional diagnosis floating amongst them — namely that pregnant women shouldn't intercourse when they're pregnant — when all the current literature suggests the contrary, that it *is* advisable to intercourse when you're pregnant, a colorful old card among us exclaiming that it actually gets the old mud flowing in a pregnant woman, who, in particular, should be forbidden to travel for obvious reasons (pregnancy), despite their desire to join the non-pregnant women (also forbidden to travel) at their so-called yoga retreat in India, itself, the retreat, located in a scummy little industrial town in the south of that country (we saw the shoddy promotional brochure), a real open sewer (obviously, we said absolutely not), where some gnome in a Speedo and Rolex would be paid handsomely to spank their spandexed asses while our country is at *war*, as if they, the Women's Auxiliary for *Peace*, for Christ's sake, somehow missed the memo that it wasn't *us* who plotted and executed such heinous acts, that we aren't the bad guys here, that it was *them* (terrorists), and people are dying, so sure, maybe we should just all up and escape to some clit-flicking commune, though that's perhaps taking things a bit too far, especially the introduction of sarcasm to the conversation, sure to pique the ire of the women who are bound to interject at this point, asking for some clarity from the odd asshole among us who said it — the

clit-flicking commune remark — that is, if the odd asshole among us could agree to call words by their particular, proper nouns, if that were possible, inasmuch as it's called an *ashram*, actually, not to get too technical about it, and thus would begin a pretty hot dressing-down, requiring us to take the initiative and quickly deploy a well-reasoned reply based on objective information in order to defend ourselves against it, the attack, it (the defense), informed by the research we're compiling on the subject vis-à-vis some useful Internet resources, bi-weekly briefings from our representative at marriage counseling and the information gathered by various other informants and operators, resulting, for instance, in what's commonly termed *a mediating response*, something along the lines that the physiological and psychological benefits of yoga are not at issue here, however important these benefits might be, because, we'll continue, if we've learned anything, we should have learned to value one another and that life is fragile, a position that is inarguably spot-on, so much so that it will back the women — wholly incapable as they are of the thought of losing an argument — into a corner from which they might well restate their impending vow of celibacy, a vow particularly hilarious coming from the pregnant women, who, despite their condition, have also been participating in the forwarding of a mass-mailer put out by some organization that bills itself as the Women's World Wide Peace Movement (WWW.PM), subject line *No Peace, No Pussy,* at which point we, for our part, might reiterate the general advice on the matter, that despite the women's evidently poor behavior at this juncture, it's nonetheless important for us to value one standing by her convictions, that otherwise speech is just so much flatulence, and, thus relenting, we could actually turn the tables on the Thumbtack (and those she represents) at the meeting by taking a page out of the women's playbook and own up to (before she's able to attack

our ignorance in having) a certain deficiency in the skills required for simply sitting down and talking, clearly accepting that we have this deficiency, explaining that restlessness in the face of gravity is a part of who we generally are, noting the fact that we've already been amply and often criticized for it by the women, but the stunning, jaw-dropping irony is that we are *here*, sitting down and talking, while she, the Thumbtack, herself, and the rest of her group seem hell-bent on flitting around the world at the first chance they get (in other words, being anything but stationary and still), indicating to us, as a matter of fact, that for them stillness takes a great deal of mental effort — obviously one cannot sit still if one is so, what's the word, *perturbed* — a rhetorical maneuver, sure, and one cobbed right out of their beloved *Introductory Guide to the Sutras* that will undoubtedly infuriate the Thumbtack, knocking the legs out from under her, so to speak, deflating her much touted superior skills at sitting still and

calmly talking, a claim made with a false sense of
calm superiority shared by all of them, as if they
were *coached*, for god's sake, when they first
announced their intention of going to India, the
announcement itself given in the darkness of our
living rooms, their sitting motionless on
cumbersomely deep-seated cushions in postures
implying great seriousness, variously looming in
the darkness across from us, putting their faces
directly into our faces, informing us of their
insanely irresponsible ambitions, ambitions so
irresponsible that we were too dumbfounded to
respond, but, believe us, if we hadn't been struck
stupid, we would've told them what we're now,
after suffering the imposition of having to take on
all this yoga business, prepared to tell the
Thumbtack, taking her on in her own terms,
arguing that if the yogi, as Patanjali himself says
(*zing*), realizes that the knower, the instrument of
knowing and the known are one, himself, the
seer, then all of us sitting here in this meeting are

already, practically speaking, yogis (never try to bullshit a bullshitter), to which she might repeat the talking points (undoubtedly originating from her) we've already heard individually from the other women in the Club, that all they want is an opportunity to get away for a little while, to remove themselves, however briefly, in order to fully inhabit their denunciation of all the bad stuff going on (we'll remind her here that five weeks is *not* a brief amount of time), a position on the predicament that we'll say we totally understand, because (wait for it) we ourselves are sensitive to and also struggle with the five kinds of mental modifications (page three of the *Introductory Guide*), themselves classified as either painful or painless, including right knowledge, misconception, verbal delusion, sleep and memory, an usurpation of knowledge that will force Thumbtack, sensing that her own weapons have been turned fully against her now, to get her hackles up and say that the women are adults who are free to make their own choices and that they're going, so how, she might ask, do we like these bananas, and after a purposeful pause here, lengthy and contemplative, we might respond that Patanjali says an image that arises on hearing mere words without any reality as its basis is verbal delusion — as in, for example, the statement that his (Patanjali's) mother was a barren woman, or when in the shadows of twilight one sees a coiled rope and mistakes it for a snake, or when an emotional depth charge is called a bunch of bananas — perhaps prompting her in the knowledge of her inevitable defeat (made more painful as it comes from within) to beg for some reasonableness in finding a compromise, a request we're more than happy to honor, because only in compromise are we able to tend to the greater good — we hardly need to remind her here of the fact that at least one of the women is in the process of applying for her green card, and as consequence, immigration would interpret her departure as a violation of the requisite probationary period — a

summation of fact that might cause Thumbtack to reply that said applicant has already given her blessing to them, the women who are going, for safe travels, and, in return, promises of some good souvenirs, and that the Patanjali quotes notwithstanding (mostly spit up here wrongly, she'll charge, in a last ditch effort to find solid ground), we really don't have any idea whatsoever what we're talking about (it's a terrible dilemma, attempting an appeal to reason with the unreasonable), a claim that we'll beg to differ with, considering that we've been working the yoga problem in general on and off ever since it surfaced, and that the preliminary findings are finally now starting to come together as our own sort of general introduction to their obsession, an increasingly unavoidable impediment, obviously, all this yoga (*union* [n], or to *yoke* [v]) business, its ancient instruction manual translated from the Sanskrit, written in the form of sutras — the Sanskrit word *sutra* being the English *thread*, such that *sutures* derive from sutras — comprising *The Yoga Sutras of Patanjali* (roughly summarized, the whole kit and caboodle, as when the restraint of mental modifications is achieved, one has reached the goal of yoga, that one can not learn from one's history, because history is an illusion, that history itself is the accumulation of unfulfilled desires, that what we want to do is stop wanting, that this desire too is a want, that therefore history repeats itself, etc.), which Hindi historians apparently date from 2500 to 2200 years old, all except one Mister Sri Swami (*person of knowledge* [n], no more, no less) Satchidanada of the Satchidanada Ashram (Yogaville, Virginia), who dates the sutras at 7000 to 2300 years old (although he is suspected by his peers of exaggerating in order to elevate his own situation), the inability of historians to pin down a more precise date for the origin of *The Yoga Sutras* in general evidently attributable to a controversy involving whether Patanjali was a single person or several persons working under the same title,

collaborating on the sutras over space and time, but while the debate of their authorship continues, an incontestable fact is that the aphorisms and the sutras they comprise are among our earliest formal compositions, that written language itself originated in Mesopotamia around 3200 B.C., and that Eastern philosophy is fundamentally the same as Western philosophy but that Eastern philosophy is dressed more colorfully, so to speak (in *saris*, someone points out), inasmuch as one of the most recent and influential practitioners of (Western) aphorisms is the Austrian philosopher Ludwig Wittgenstein, in particular his *Tractatus Logico-Philiosophicus*, wherein Wittgenstein's use of aphorisms is valued by the editors of the *Complete Encyclopedia of Western Philosophical Thought* for being *completely and utterly revealing*, as if each of Wittgenstein's aphorisms is Wittgenstein himself reaching into his rough woolen trousers, slapping his scrotum onto the table for examination in order that we may contemplate each vein, each minute wrinkle, hair, the very follicle from which each hair sprouts, and while we are of course free to reject any one of Wittgenstein's propositions out of hand, Wittgenstein can assert that each atomic fact contains within it all atomic facts, to which we can say nice try, Ludwig, but we don't *think* so (and still it's unnerving to find one so open, we read, his overtures so bald, his posture so defenseless, his angular countenance so unclouded, his sullen cheeks a little rouged), thereby leaving him to his own devices, just sitting there on his threadbare, faded pink Queen Ann in a windowless room, listening to Mahler's *Das Lied von der Erde* while simultaneously recalling two youths from his boyhood who are leading two horses grazing, themselves (horses) on the white and purple lilies growing sporadically on the side of the road — one of the boys leading one of the horses, Wittgenstein confesses, is himself — a reverie accompanied by the music he's listening to so that the gramophone record of the symphony,

Wittgenstein says, the musical thought, the score, the waves of sound, are all inside one simultaneously, so that the gramophone record, the musical thought, the score, the waves of sound, contain each other's logical structure, Wittgenstein says, just as the two youths, their two horses and their lilies are assembled by identical atomic facts, thus concluding that they are all in a certain sense one, a claim that might inspire some to tell Wittgenstein to stop harassing us here, to say unambiguously that we flatly reject his advancements — that no means *no*, Ludwig — but if we do reject any one of his propositions, his whole gesture then groans under the weight of its collapsing structure, leaving poor Wittgenstein with his rough woolen trousers slung around his ankles, his decisiveness shriveled, drained of all that so-called bold blood, inching its way back toward the spine of his treatise, his plaintive, wondering eyes searching behind us for the source of his shame, a shame central to both Western and

Eastern philosophies alike, it's pointed out, so that while there's not complete consensus on the dates of the Patanjali documents, most swamis in general do seem unified against what they see as the subversive ego, this infamous *I* of ours, described variously as a Velcro to pleasure, swooning diva in pain, terrified Box Terrier snarling at death, clinging sloth to the tree of life, and therefore source of our misery, the countervailing position of this misery being death, swamis say, pansy, because *I* am a big fat pansy, swamis say, and the pansy's bed, the sky where the pansies bloom, a #2 sheet rock screw lodged in a steel-belted Firestone Wilderness radial tire, the tire itself, the truck, an accumulation of things that we call ourselves, though in truth our lives are inferential, swamis say, illusory, because in fact we are all of us a steaming pile of spoor from which we are to infer the animal browsing conifers in the blue silence of a cold winter night, the conifers themselves, the animal, the blue silence, the

winter, the cold, all of it dished up in so-called aphorisms, their restrictions giving the *appearance* of being maddeningly logical, wherein the idea is apparently supposed to be like an animal, the form a mode of tracking so that if the hunter becomes lost, we learn, he can presumably retrace his steps backward, or then again there's an argument to be made that maybe it's supposed to work like subjecting one's mind to a slow drip of Professional Strength Liquid Plumber that, employed as a caustic agent, is apparently designed to burn through the clog of unenlightened consciousness (or maybe it's meant to be like a cough drop lozenge, so that we're to suck on this for awhile, the notion that yoga is the cessation of movements in the consciousness, and other dopey platitudes that make you cough when you say them) to the extent that enlightenment is what's purported to be left there in the scarred, empty casing of our skulls, but in order to receive the full benefit of this accumulated acid bath, we cannot skip from aphorism A to aphorism C in the sutra sequence A B C, for instance, because without the progression through aphorism B, the sutra itself apparently becomes more sewage in the sinkhole of our unenlightened minds — hippies having assigned mass to it, determining that it's heavy — a mind awash in sorrow and despondency, a sorrow manifesting itself in tears, the act of excessively wiping them (tears) away producing conjunctivitis, a bacterial infection of the eye (in other words, the bacterium breeding on the organically rich surface of those limpid pools creates the combustive burning and itching), the treatment involving two drops of sulfacetamide sodium applied directly to the infected eye every six to eight hours, such that, if the afflicted follows this sutra to the letter, she will be cured of what ails her, hence what's believed to be the prescriptive, utilitarian power of the sutra, wherein the problem is stated and the problem is resolved, sans baseless whining, without bullshitting around, but rather breaking

things down to manageable steps instead of trying to account for the whole mess (to be honest, we're all for that), some two thousand five hundred years of recorded despair dumped into the present, neither an easily manageable amount of time nor despondency, believe us, despite what some swamis would have us believe, when, really, swamis are just like the rest of us — in fact *are us*, simply, by definition again, *people of knowledge* — such that some swamis make it their business to provide the notation of a remainder in a long division problem as *r*, while others provide the largest export crop of Brazil, expressed in kilotons, and decree that the most effective rhetoric for baking a bundt cake is process analysis, to say nothing of the numerous State-supported swamis who locate their ashrams in Departments of Motor Vehicles and Natural Recourses, patiently answering untold questions posed to them from the great, faceless petitioner, either withholding or granting licenses, depending, as when it (the great, faceless petitioner) is idiotically applying for a permit to burn in the dry months of fall (we can't allow it to burn), or applying to own the water in a steam cutting through its land (it can't own the water), or as when it's attempting to reserve a campsite at the Happy Glenn Campground, it's suddenly incumbent upon us to point out the obvious, that the Happy Glenn Campground no longer exists, the memories of the petitioner notwithstanding, whose happiest memories, we're told, are inextricably associated with the Happy Glenn Campground (it might well exist in the memory, we say, but it no longer exists in this particular, so to speak, state), and that things just don't disappear, to which we might respond that things might be presently reduced to a rusting trash barrel and precisely the land it still sits on, itself, the barrel, scheduled for removal ten minutes ago, a fact that the petitioner might tell us we should be ashamed of, causing us to ask that the good citizen listen up, because the fact is that

one's memory is neither recognized as an article of
nature nor natural resource, so the Department of
Natural Resources is no more responsible for the
caretaking of the *matériel* of the petitioner's
nostalgia than it is for the evisceration of a DNR
employee's simple, clean and good desire of
making it one's life's work the study of muskrat
traffic patterns on the frozen marsh — the
mapping of their throughways between reedy
berms of dry land, the tracing of the boarders of
their ghettos on the open ice — in order to achieve
an understanding of muskrat society far and above
one's ability to understand one's own, however
contemptible that may be at present, as opposed to
that life so clearly (and cleanly) understood and
lived in a splendiferously snow-white solitude
(inhabiting us as we inhabit it), until such time
such studies and activities are deemed superfluous,
forcing a situation where one's many talents are
instead better put to use in doing its (the DNR's)
administrative bidding, a declaration that might

prompt the petitioner to assert that it pays our salary, goddamnit, a disclosure of contract inspiring us to point to the fact that gophers and kangaroo rats have underground rooms in their tunnels serving as latrines, and in the drier country of the Southwest, packrat middens may be coated with scat and urine deposits dating back thousands of years, leading us to our point here, specifically that we aren't paid enough to both have the knowledge of that mystery and continue this conversation, the thrust of which, taken as a whole — the bare gist of it, we mean — is admittedly a little more flowery and meandering than most of us are prepared for, but nonetheless brings full circle the force of the argument against falsely elevating the social position of swamis, an argument, furthermore (at least judging by the considerable silence proceeding it), that seems uniformly accepted in an extended, thought-filled pause, until someone finally breaks in with a weather check — presently 47 degrees Fahrenheit,

an unseasonably warm December day — noting also that the pressure is falling, an Arctic front forecast to barrel down from Alberta, Canada, bringing with it blizzard conditions overnight, an eventuality that is hard to believe at the moment, what with the sky a dim blue, the air uncommonly thick and soft as if one's head were in a box of cotton, a silence in fact so thick that someone remarks that one could almost hear the oncoming snow, a remark that someone suggests should include the phrase *baleful moaning*, an amendment that gets a lot of laughs out loud before we switch gears and get down to a matter a little closer to home, the DNR's requisition order for a new server, the keystone to our possible adult entertainment enterprise, a CP 750 Whisper stalled somewhere in the State's approval process, suggesting a long wait indeed (take a request for a copier repair order, and quadruple it, times a factor of ten), when all the while the thing's just sitting there as an idea, gathering flies, so to speak, instead of being plugged in, the argument goes, powered-up and used to get enough cash flow going to roll over and purchase *another* dedicated server to replace the one just sitting there (as an idea, still gathering flies), so that we could already have two instead of just the one just sitting there, draped in a canvas drip cloth in the center of the old, purple mailroom that Maintenance is preparing to repaint (their third attempt, for god's sake) in mauve by mixing Ravishing Red (leftover from the Fire Department's 4th of July float) with Hypnotic Blue (leftover from the DMV's road-salt storage facility) and lightening it, for the third time, with more Ice White (excess ceiling paint found in storage), when everyone knows that it's the cost of the labor, not the cost of the stupid paint itself that determines the budget of such a project, but whatever, we mean, we're suddenly the landed gentry, house rich and cash poor as the saying goes, a bunch of penny-pinching morons trying to save money by mixing leftover paint, all

us still secretly burning from our Pension Manager
missing the opportunity to buy Microsoft stock
when some friend of a friend of a friend said buy
back when they, Microsoft (what a name), had just
a couple of hundred employees, representing one
opportunity among a hundred missed opportunities
that — here we can't help but think of intermittent
windshield wipers wiping the windshield right
before our eyes, slow and steady, dragging
themselves back and forth, back and forth, slowly
— pass before our eyes, which we just can't seem
to see (take Yahoo, for example, because we
didn't), to say nothing of all the other stuff that the
really smart, miraculously placed son of a bitches
already know about but are keeping under wraps
through various distractions, as in, not to sound
too conspiratorial, the whole clocks resetting
fiasco, that whole Y2K business about a memory
conniption coming from mixing up the 0s and 1s
in the code that the doomsayers said was going to
cause Armageddon at the turn of the millennium,

a carefully crafted, orchestrated distraction (from exactly what, we'll probably never know), as if one catastrophe could outweigh and detract from the other in an endless series of distracting catastrophes, the problem here being of course that the clocks resetting catastrophe was nothing, no matter how much everybody wanted it to be more, but it was a distraction nonetheless, one that doubtlessly played right into the hands of the real movers and shakers of this world, who probably hatched the very plan that distracted us long enough for the next big thing to be brought into the world, so that by the time the thing is obviously right in front of us (whatever that thing might be — Google), it's already a little too late for the rest of us, but, by god, not this time, we say, no, despite the predictable resistance we might meet, especially by that faction in their hemp bloomers who'll undoubtedly stop their breathing exercises and who knows what else long enough to try and stand between us and a four

billion dollar a year industry, speaking of which
— hemp bloomers and organic cotton socks —
take your basic refrigerator packing material, cut
it up into six foot sections and sell it for twenty-
five bucks a piece as a so-called sticky mat that
costs basically nothing to begin with, wow, now
there's a racket that we should've bought into in the
first place, speaking of fiscal responsibility, of
getting in when the getting's good, meaning we're
late to the on-line adult entertainment party
already, but the party's still going if we can just
think our way through the latest, biggest headache,
principally the processing of financial transactions
by third party vendors who obviously want their
cut, enviably positioned, as they are, between
source and consumer, a location that one can't
blame them for staking out, seeing it's a free
market economy and that the opportunity was
there (though we were obviously too distracted by
something else to see it ourselves), but surely, if a
push of the button can empty out the entire

airspace of the continental U.S. of A, there
certainly must be another way to process a $21.50
membership fee, a simple problem that probably
has an equally simple solution, if we could just find
a quiet moment to think it through, free from
distractions and petty foolishness, like the
unnecessary confusion caused by some of the
women calling one another by different names, to
give just one recent example, a name the
Thumbtack apparently assigned to them —
Suprita or Spirolina or Spatula — so that when the
women speak to one another on the phone it
sounds like they're kibitzing about some far-flung
stranger, someone's old aunt packed in mothballs
in Toledo, not themselves, that this Velveeta
actually refers to a Julie, whose perfectly good
English name we've known pretty much all our
lives, prompting one of us to ask the rationale
behind the changing of the names in the first place,
and having not received a sufficient answer (read:
any answer at all), asking that they knock it off

because it makes no sense — besides being deeply annoying — and now that we're on the subject, we might use *this* opportunity to inform them that their trip to India is indefinitely canceled due to the war declared upon us, an unforeseen change of circumstances (however cataclysmic) which the travel industry itself no doubt comprehends so perhaps will refund all, or at least part of the money paid them (travel agents), because they're not going, the women, they really aren't, we'll say, prepared for a humdinger of an argument per earlier scenario, possibly even screaming, or maybe something more, something physical, perhaps, anything but the silent treatment, hopefully, that spooky, unnerving stillness that makes us quietly back out of the room and take temporary refuge in the garage to listen to, say, the Giants playing the Packers on the radio while drinking a few beers and sorting screws, biding time, waiting out a night of low- to moderate-levels of tension, stewing over the possible significance of the numerous incidents of excessive cleaning that are beginning to call attention to themselves, how the dinner table is cleared while the last crumb falls, how there's never a dirty dish that isn't already done, air drying in the dish rack, how closets are suddenly reorganized, all of them, each and every one, the stubborn hard water deposits on the shower miraculously vanished (as have the contents of the junk drawer), or how the drapes are dustless, the floors shine, the carpet always damp from a recent steam cleaning, all coming as no surprise, actually — we're used to it at certain times of the month, particularly right before the full moon — until reports start circulating about how some of the women have been caught tilting their heads sideways so that they can insert the spout of a miniature teapot into their nostrils, specifically pouring warm salt water into the upper nostril, blowing it out the lower, rinsing and repeating, or how packaging found in the garbage suggests the increased use of

self-administered enemas, or the incidents of several of the (non-pregnant) women caught vomiting in the morning *on purpose*, vomiting induced by drinking several glasses of what's described as saline water on an empty stomach, retching it into the toilet, or how a few of them have been seen performing so-called food-pipe cleansing by swallowing what's described as approximately ten foot strips of cotton chord soaked in milk, then pulling it, the chord, out again, followed by drinking the glass of milk, or finally how, of particular concern, a couple of the women have been caught red-handed *drinking* their own urine, an activity as unacceptable as it is revolting, but all attempts at intervention are met with confrontation, sometimes confrontations that include objects actually being thrown, including coffee cups, toothbrushes, clothes hampers, the dirty clothes exploding on the bathroom floor, after which the women root through the debris, all those dirty clothes, calling

us dirty animals, saying there isn't enough time or
bleach in the world to keep a man's underpants
clean, picking a more worn pair from the heap and
waiving it in our face like a flag to our own
embarrassment, when, to be fair, the underwear
under consideration are never the newest nor
cleanest example in our repertoire, followed then
by their snatching up the dirty T-shirts with
yellow perspiration quarter-moons staining the
armpits — these are thrown at us too — until
they finally gain control of their senses, telling us
to buy black underwear from now on, or dark blue
ones, or any color other than the filthy white ones,
a concession we say that we are more than happy
to make, when in truth it's just another in a long,
long, long list of concessions that we feel we've
been making and keeping pretty close track of in
an effort to regain some calm in these situations,
incidents so stressful we're forced to try to burn
through them by taking a brisk walk in the night,
and if that doesn't work, if stress becomes panic,

there's the quick-dissolve dose of Clonazepam to consider, but this needs to be considered sooner in the stress-related event than later, ideally *before* the onset of the panic event, meaning preemptively, meaning the use of the Clonazepam has to be administered, in the words of the prescriber, *prophylactically*, requiring a certain measure of self-care, we're told, an understanding of when, however subconsciously, one's own best interests are under attack by one's own self, despite, as the women charge, one's apparent inability to identify moments when one's own best interest are under attack by one's self, as if the stress itself is just another terrorist (the panic attacks themselves are particularly terrifying), who, those terrorists, we primarily blame for the stress in the first place, the terrorists and the looming budget crisis and the general low-level anxiety involved in starting our adult entertainment business venture to address our paltry First Responders funding, a viscid vein of stress admittedly producing some undeniably appalling examples of self-care of late, like the one involving the dragging out of a big red cooler from the garage into the late Autumn sunlight, filling it with ice and a 12 pack of Coors before noon in order to scrape and prime the trim on the house, an example that ends an hour and a half later with a fall from the ladder, down into the hydrangeas, just then in full bloom, now crushed, now totally ruined by the amount of beer consumed in the example, though, fortunately, there's still enough ice left in the bottom of the cooler to fill a large Ziploc bag, the very need for which earns one a big F-minus on the self-care report card, as writhing on the dining room floor with a dislocated shoulder decidedly does *not* project the image of self-care, to say nothing of the subsequent passing out on the dining room floor from the pain, an injury directly traceable and caused by the stress at work created by those Arabs attacking our homeland, resulting in our need for land surveys in order to identify topographically appropriate

emergency staging areas, complete with triage
tents equipped with the requisite number of
cotton compresses for a finite number of potential
victims, extrapolated as a percentage of population,
to say nothing of the need to figure out a way to
financially support said staging areas and cotton
compresses, a conundrum that screams our need
to get *something* up and working to generate
positive cash flow to acquire these staples,
requiring us to go out there and get fishing for it,
throwing our bait, watching what nibbles on the
bait, charting the interested hits, documenting
the numbers of passers-by, so that if no one is
swallowing we change baits, throwing a little *deep
throat* action out there if need be, and if that doesn't
work, a little *blond nubile deep throat* action,
switching things around, a little *missionary* now
and then to catch the so-called traditionalists,
despite the fact there's reportedly no such thing to
speak of anymore, meaning that pool's reportedly
run pretty well bone-dry, at least according to our

own research, itself growing so comprehensive that there's been talk of late that what we should actually do is sell what we know, moving therefore at one remove into consulting, giving seminars to other municipalities, perhaps, where we would say how happy we are to be here with you to talk about interfaces, Web hosting and the whatnot, that this is really exciting venue for us, wherever this venue might be (here we loosely follow the program, the program's template, rather, that one of us lately survived firsthand when accompanying his wife to one of *her* own seminars) and that we're especially excited, we mean you can count on us to hang back for the Hindi iconography in Led Zeppelin lyrics, as what comes after the lunch break, followed by something about the meaning of breathing and the right ways of jumping, because we were really big fans of the Led Zeppelin lyrics, way back before we got married, when we were just a bunch of snot-nosed teenagers, so really, this is our lucky, lucky day, to say nothing

about the breathing, but as for jumping, we're not so sure, but okay, we're willing to learn a little something here today, too, insofar as jumping is concerned, which more than indicates that the program has worn out its usefulness here as a template for our own program, and that we might do well to simply move on to today's topic, how it's common knowledge in certain circles that the platforms available to us at the Department of Natural Resources — as well as those operated by most State and Federal agencies for that matter — provide an abundance of feral spaces for the development of commercial Internet sites for adult entertainment purposes, opportunities generated by the government's tendency to both invest in surpluses and to think about communication traffic as a measure of volume (i.e., *bigness*), resulting in the incontestable fact that the United States government has unwittingly become the largest exporter of Internet pornography in the entire world, and while we aren't at liberty to disclose the exact location of the DNR we're referring to here, we also don't want to seem too cagey, either, and threaten the practical gist of the information, although to be perfectly clear, we're not talking *piracy* but *opportunity*, an opportunity that for all its potential has become a tricky business, perpetually in transition, unmoored from its own recent history, even, wherein, historically speaking, Internet pornography sites made their profit exclusively by selling subscriptions to content, representing the glory days of the industry before the worrisome trend — we worry about this all the time, believe us — that much in the same way gas station owners don't make their money from the pump but from the overpriced sundries sold as conveniences, adult entertainment sites are being made to rely more and more on the sale of various male enhancement and sexual performance drugs, as well as an array of prosthetic devices, primarily vaginas of a synthetic material, assorted vibrators

and your classic dildos, and, adding to these facts, is the reality that competition for consumers now dictates that much of the content they once were required to purchase in the past is made available for free in so-called promotional material, a policy decision fueled in part by advertising revenue (another crucial profit source), based as it is on the amount of traffic through a given site, not on the quality of the consumer's experience (the hit's a cash register ring, people, remember that), all of which contributes to the cumulative frustrations the upstart webmaster should expect to confront in such places as our local DNR, to take our example, because the DNR is decidedly *not* a warehouse facility, naturally, and that accumulating and processing large amounts of merchandise (constituting roughly 30% of net profit at present, though diminishing) would undoubtedly call attention to one's self and such ancillary enterprises, but despite these frustrations, we believe that there is no better time to get into the

business, principally because the attack on the
United States of America has contributed to the
upsurge in Internet traffic to adult entertainment
sites, themselves witnessing triple-digit growth in
the quarter beginning September and ending this
past November, a trend that should be of surprise
to no one, considering that Americans are
becoming increasingly bored with the excessive
amount of time they are spending at home —
restaurant receipts are down a dismal 11.6%
nationwide — and also because pornography in
general has been shown to relieve stress, the
stress-reducing effects having been long established
in the scientific community (idea: pop-up survey
asking consumer to comment on motive for
visiting à la Travelocity) despite the downward
pressure on the industry coming from those who
hold tenaciously to their non-masturbatory
prohibitions, those who we view as promoting
non-masturbatory mythologies, meaning all the
available studies show if a male individual in

particular (but by no means exclusively) is put in a room with a computer for a week, and if said individual is assured privacy, the first thing the individual is going to do is email, and the second thing that individual is going to do is access a little Internet pornography, a fact as true in Atlanta as it is in Zimbabwe, so that the patterns of our inquiries and searching appear exactly identical, regardless of culture, a pattern, furthermore, that should catch no one off guard, because as much as the content of the Internet and its usage is made from our minds, it's hard to deny we're not of the same mind (pause for laughter), regardless of culture, except for the Japanese, who are, statistically speaking, the most undersexed people in the world, and also the largest consumers of Internet pornography in the world (do the math), so in summary, first we want to talk, then we want to see a little skin, in that order, and the rest of our Internet usage — everything from shopping to research — is summarily dwarfed by email and porn, a truth we are not here to apologize for, but instead are here to remind you all, who said it, somebody famous, that all of it — the movies, the books, the songs on the radio, the paintings, the TV shows — all of it is about three things — birth, sex, and death — that in other words we're born, we shoot our wad, and then we fall down and die, and in between we do a lot of talking and thinking about these things (although we probably wouldn't use the phrase *shoot our wad*, per se), so as far as we're concerned, the sex act itself as offered by your basic Internet adult entertainment provider offers the whole production in miniature, where one experiences a little foreplay, a little rising and heating up of the action, the climax at the climax, as it were, and then the satisfied sleep, for which, again, we offer no apologies, because to apologize would be to fabricate an apology for the way we are, how we're built, to say nothing of the fact that we're *entertainment* providers, not *dictators*, and now, in closing, we could distribute some

tasteful brochures, ones with the slots cut in them for business cards to be kept in a Rolodex on another Mayor's desk even if the brochure advertising our service was inadvertently tossed aside, ensuring that the Mayor, or one of the Mayor's delegates, could contact us in an effort to identify as-yet undisclosed, extraordinarily lucrative profit centers to tap into in order to meet the basic human needs of the Mayor's constituency, or, on the other hand (as the counterargument goes), a Mayor might decide to forego the problems of Web hosting as laid out here entirely and instead invest directly into the *creation of content*, a production like the one now floated, entitled *Physical Therapy*, wherein a patient receives home visits for carpal tunnel syndrome (as an aside, OSHA deems the affliction an occupational injury, one sustained from repetitive tasks, so its treatment is *supposed* to be funded by Workman's Compensation), though its creator indicates that he's not married to carpal tunnel syndrome,

offering as alternative suggestions a herniated disk
between L4 and L5 (car accident), or basic, various
replacements — hip (a fall), knee (on the court),
elbow (freak shopping cart accident) — perhaps
even a case of TMJ, causing the actor's jaw to be
wired shut (no motive given, just a crummy
genetic predisposition), making it a silent
production, at least on his end, which might make
things pretty interesting when the physical
therapist arrives at the door, described as a super
hot babe in a nurse's outfit, who's not here to help
us into the bathroom to take a leak, not *this* time,
but she *is* going to make us feel better with some
physical therapy that, on second thought, the
creator reconsiders, actually might begin in the
bathroom after all with some hot soaping-up
action in the shower, followed by a basic massage
that turns into *something more* because she knows
where you hurt and how to *make you feel better*,
straddling the bad cases who are not ambulatory,
hiking up her short skirt, grinding her pelvis into

our back (ouch), getting pretty worked up —
there's the requisite moaning and groaning here,
we're told — turning the patient over so the *real*
physical therapy can begin, asking if she's found
the spot that ails us, a question generating the one-
word response (or in the case of TMJ, gesture)
lower, lower, *lower*, at which point things get *crazy*
with all sorts of possibilities for all kinds of hot
physical therapy action in all kinds of physically
therapeutic positions, because, it's clear by this
point, the guy's just *horny*, he's not really hurt, not
hurt really, but he's got physical *needs* that need
attending to, as opposed to the emotional ones,
themselves better served by entering into a
therapeutic relationship with someone versed in
the vagaries of emotional needs, like our own
marriage counselor, to give just one example, who
one of us is seeing on Mondays on behalf of us all,
mining for general marriage advice, regularly
reporting back to us such information as — this
from last Monday's session — in a long and

uncelebrated career (we're paraphrasing) one comes to the inescapable conclusion that what appears to be a spectacular occurrence is the end result of commonplace occurrences, habituated over time, going thusly unnoticed as habits are wont to do, such as an inequitable division of domestic labor, which is a biggie, insofar as while one might *think* housework is divided pretty equitably in the home, the other spouse might beg to differ, as in the simple task of helping to do the laundry — it's an interesting word, *help* — whereby one spouse might ask for *help* with the laundry when, in fact, the other spouse, meaning the spouse asked, actually ends up doing *all* the laundry (*help,* therefore, becoming a covert term to avoid doing any laundry), and the dishes, too, meaning the breakfast dishes, lunch dishes *and* the dinner dishes, for example, or one might do the drying of the clothes but not the washing of the clothes, so in point of fact one is not doing the laundry *in toto*, inasmuch as the laundry requires both the washing *and* the drying of the clothes, all of it unavoidably leading us to our point, the marriage counselor is reported as having said, that a marriage is a negotiation, wherein one spouse might have a thing about drying the clothes, the same thing the same spouse has about washing silverware, something about the sound of metal on metal — forks against spoons, zippers against the dryer drum — that, the spouse swears, *hurts the teeth*, so that this same spouse might volunteer to dry the previously washed clothes, but fuck it, the clothes must be *folded* for the laundry to be *done*, properly speaking, so perhaps the same spouse also gets roped into doing that, too, never minding for the moment that a sink full of silverware means that the dishes haven't been *washed*, properly speaking, so perhaps this same spouse gets roped into doing that, too, in a model that seems increasingly less democratic, unless the other spouse offers to even the playing field and fold the clothes democratically, a gesture entailing one spouse folding the other spouse's clothes and perhaps anything else that happens to need folding, despite what the other spouse might say about shirking housework, whose own clothes are almost precious in their smallness, as when holding them up to the light, it's impossible not to be moved while folding them, the clothes, themselves seeming so occasionally small that it's difficult to believe they fit a full-grown adult human being, all these little shirts, the little pants and washable skirts, the size of the panties, some of them cotton, some of them silk, some with faded stripes, some of them slippery, shiny and new, all of them deeply moving in their extraordinarily vulnerable, solitary (occasionally seeming) smallness, a sentiment deemed by the marriage counselor as operative (re: vulnerability), because in the face of it all, in both our general anxiety and our singular fear of the violent attacks sure to come, what the women surely want are some basic assurances, some simple, basic assurance that if they find themselves falling from a burning building, for example, if the flames and smoke behind them are so unbearably intense that the only decision is to jump, they need reassurance that we will be there, despite pervasive fears of heights, despite every anxiety dream of being stranded on high, unstable places, that all our affections will be marshaled in resisting the most deeply felt and primitive impulse to let go and hide our face with the fingers of our hands before impact, regardless of how futile this gesture would be, to just hold on even if we're such a great distance from the ground that we're twisting in the wind above or below each other for a full six or seven seconds, depending on cross winds, causing our shoulders to be ripped from their sockets, that we will nonetheless keep holding onto each other through this agony of pain, that finally, given all of this, we will not let each other go and, in not letting go, therefore earn the right to be included in such noble examples, but even before an affirmative response can be formulated to all of this, the marriage counselor requests (through our intermediary) that we take a step back and interpret our actions, to think of one's self and one's actions as assembled matters of unadorned facts, as if the self was a near-distance object available, consequently, for an objective assessment (okay, we think we got it), causing us to think here of the incident at Lamaze class last Sunday involving one of us sitting on a blanket, his pregnant wife reclining between his legs, his hands cupped around her swollen belly trying to feel the subtle movement, the little twitter and thrum promised there, and how, entirely unprovoked, he had a sudden and violent urge to stand up to challenge any other man in the room who would do him and his harm, and how this same young man, thinking the scenario through, imagined himself a gaping silence after delivering it, his declaration, earnestly speechless afterwards, but soldiering on toward a speakable language in the layers of images just then flooding through his mind (i.e., professional research hazard), including, he recounted to us, unbelievable amounts of fluid erupting like geysers from various vaginas (as a newly emergent category, a marketing preoccupation he had already subdivided between shaved and unshaved sources), plus mountains of limbs and various shadows on inestimable amounts of flesh, including bottomless, black orifices — anal, oral, vaginal, orbital — all thinly veiled in a fog of smoke, through which we could clearly see his point of view and the uncomfortable truths located therein, as in his supremely uncomfortable revelation that the so-called bikini wax indulges a man's pedophilic fantasies, or his opinion that the aggressively baggy clothes worn by our young people of late is an attempt to be seen as infantile, children playing dress up in big people's clothes and therefore not responsible for their increasingly unglued lives (well, he said, it's time for them to grow up, the little shits), and that ultimately gestation has been the subject of all the near-born babies with or without his or any of our elaboration, so that we had to admit it, okay, that some of us needed to shut up a little bit more and do some listening, to *hear* the women's (pregnant or not) concerns, agreeing to take the following measures preemptively, well before the women raise them in the first place, including no longer considering cross-posting material from *Captain Stabbin'*, with its claim (albeit gimmicky and undoubtedly staged) that the *crew* is thrown overboard after *getting it in the end*, that we pledge to be forever closed to the *Pregnant Moms* category, as well as to all forms of bestiality and any suggestion whatsoever to minors, including the simple designation *17*, causing some of us to consider joining Big Brothers in an effort to generate some positive self-esteem in our more wayward, baggy youths, and, most importantly, from this point forward that we seriously consider withdrawing our representative from marriage counseling, whose increasingly esoteric gibberish seems more and more of a waste

of time and resources, and instead allocate said
resources to planting another mole amongst the
women in order to divine their overall mood and
to get to the bottom of their activities, although,
admittedly, this will be more difficult considering
the cover of our previous informant was blown,
despite his success at infiltrating their twice-daily
activities by expressing a keen and sincere interest
in taking up yoga — his bursitis here cited, an
arthritic knee — so that he arrived late at his first
class (something about a real estate closing
dragging on) and, unfortunately, left early
(conspicuously slinked out, truth be told, under
the discerning and watchful gaze of the women),
but still, regardless of his brief foray, we believe
we   acquired   enough   boots-on-the-ground
information to get the gist of the thing, the general
milieu,   which   involved   Thumbtack   wearing
something appearing to be a diaper, instructing
her students to get into something called the
mountain pose, telling them that we in our

foolishness want to go to the mountain tops, but that she wanted them to *show* her these mountains, to *be* these mountains by standing with feet together, hands at the sides, eyes looking forward like the hermit the students so wrongly idolized on the mountain top, looking out on some horizon, when instead it was time to turn that gaze inward and see — evidently by spreading the toes, opening them, then putting them back down one by one as the mountain base — that we *are* the mountain itself, so breathe, people, she said, breathe your mountain breath up there in your mountaintop, way up there alone, your head in the clouds, and take this time to think about how we spend our days screaming at each other over what we see as vast distances, from mountain peak to mountain peak, when the further we go down the mountain, the closer the mountains get, so that finally on the valley floor we see that the mountains are connected, our mountain base shared by all mountain bases, the pressure behind each word that we are screaming, the pressure behind each act that we are acting as a mountain is geologic in its proportion, so vast and seemingly timeless that we cannot see it, though it must be acknowledged it is there, people, this inexorable connection, even though, from where we are looking, we cannot see it, a point of view that must be changed now, for we are not alone, and the illusion to the contrary causes such violence, a violence in us that we must change now for ourselves and for our children or, mark her words, we will most certainly raise a generation of serial killers, she said, then instructed them to strike another pose, something called the Downward Facing Hero, its benefits, she said, encompassing relief from fatigue and headache, the reduction of acidity and flatulence, the alleviation of menstrual pain and the depression associated with menstruation, so drop to your knees, she said, spread them and bend forward with your arms outstretched, the palms of your hands and forehead pressing into the

floor, as if *through* the floor, becoming as stationary
and solid *as* the floor, for the true hero, she
reportedly said, does nothing, has disassociated
herself from the pain and finds liberation in the
solidity of this silence, a silence to be breathed
into by pressing your hands and heads deeper into
the floor, she said, a bowing down through the
floor, into the ground, a giving worship to the
letting go, so that you are no longer watching the
watch, people, but now the watch is watching you,
and now bend *lower*, press harder into it, that's it,
and now lay down and prepare for Corpse Pose,
people, she said, walking around the room,
handing out long gauze bandages, saying that the
stillness is not meditation, people, but a means
toward mastery, a surrender to *that* that does not
die down in the valley, at which point the women
sat down on their mats and began wrapping their
heads in the bandages, covering their eyes, each of
them lying down after, one by one, stretching out
their legs and arms, in a posture where our man

left them as fast as he possibly could, hightailing it
out of there, to here, where he arrived not empty
handed, fortunately, having procured some of
their instructional material in a spiral bound
compendium, containing excerpts from, among
other sources, a book titled the *Upanishads*, with
its detailed, 2500-year-old instructions on how to
sit properly — how we're supposed to sit in a
secret place, in solitude, in a spot both clean and
pure, upon a seat that is firm, neither too high nor
too low, covered with layers of cloth (preferably
deerskin for some reason, if we can get our hands
on some deerskin) amidst some unspecified sacred
grasses, endeavoring to get our organs of
perception and action finally under control, trying
to stop looking over our shoulders or up into the
sky or wherever, but instead with our body, neck
and head erect, immovable and still, with our
vision indrawn, our sight fixed at the tip of our
nose, our soul at peace and fearless, we should rest
now, which evidently doesn't mean that we don't

have to stop being vigilant, but that our controlled
mind should be absorbed in the *Me*, meaning
ourselves, thus concluding the rules of sitting —
resulting in the dictum that if we're determined to
sit, we're supposed to sit *right*, and if we want to
half-ass it, we're supposed to sit somewhere else
and miss the opportunity to absorb our mind in
the peace that rests in the *Me*, etcetera, where (in
Me) we don't have to move a muscle, don't have to
lift a finger or leave this room to find it, because
it's apparently already here, waiting to be found,
despite the women's conviction that it would be
somewhat easier if they put themselves in a
different place to find it, like that shithole India,
for instance, all the way over there just to take
their so-called emotional intelligence to their
bodies, to evidently inquire into its *true* condition,
an aspect we can see clearly on their glowering
faces, prompting us to ask of them, the faces, the
nature of all this glowering, all this unhappiness,
whether it's because the garbage needs to be taken

out or the sidewalk needs salting, or if the lack of focus in their eyes betrays an emotional dissatisfaction in particular, and, if so, how, we wonder, might it help explain their wall of frigidity, because we want them to understand that, even while we're made to drop a wad down the shower drain, all thoughts are singularly upon them and them alone, forcing us to insist on our trustworthiness even as they attempt to hide their handwriting, loosely looped as crochet knots and pinned against the kitchen table with their knitting-needle forearm so that we can't help but question the content of their cryptic writing, or why, after it's revealed to us, we read *go fuck yourself* in big, knotty letters at the end of the paragraph they're laboring over, thereby emphasizing what we've concluded in other similar circumstances, that the women can be bitches, a claim, somebody points out (rightly) one doesn't make unless one is ready to take full responsibility for it, the declaration, if we're really prepared to

make it, that we've got to be prepared to *own* the ugly thrust of it, the ugly *bitch* of it in particular, the word bristling before us like a cornered porcupine, all its quill-like consonants cocked up in provocation, so that we have to recognize that what we're doing here is goading it on, trying to bait it, drawing the bitch forward, bringing it out into the light of day, an enraged, red-eyed rodent of the genus *slut* and *cunt*, such that even the words *asshole* and *douchebag*, with their more softening vowels, sound so much less abrupt and confrontational somehow, although, we admit, this isn't being sensitive to other points of view — this isn't sensitive to other points of view *at all* — but herein lies the problem, namely trying to see things from a different perspective, the promise being that we will somehow see our own situation just a little better, and yet, to be fair, in the absence of the women not being allowed to defend themselves here, a defense should be mounted on their behalf because, truthfully, they're often not painted so rosily, as on the issue of hygiene, for example, they're admonished for their pores, the butt of a joke involving how their pores are so tight, if a kid licked their foreheads on a freezing day, the kid's tongue would get stuck on their skin (still, if they hate the cold, it would be reasonable to leave the cold, a car trip down to the Gulf, not an airplane trip halfway around the world), that they're scrubbed so clean they've finally scrubbed their eyebrows off, that they operate within a conflicting aroma of astringents and Fitch's Chamomile Soap — who knows who came up with the name of the soap — all of which would undoubtedly lower their opinion of us here, not the content of what's being said, per se, but the motives for saying it, but then, they have no idea of what occurs in their absence, what we have to deal with daily, even *hourly*, as if in the last sixty minutes a new pizzeria *magically* opened up, that the dwarf screaming in falsetto for a building permit *miraculously* shut up and found some of that

so-called *inner peace*, that a cosmetics consultant *wasn't* discovered embezzling tens of thousands and investing heavily in Yen, and, while we're on the subject of policing, that they (the police), didn't find a grandmother in her bathtub in the next town over, a pillow under her head, a half-eaten chicken salad sandwich on the rim of the tub, a propane hose disconnected from her bathroom heater (for an old lady, a member of our own EMS reports, her mechanical aptitude was impressive), or that the lines everywhere are growing longer as the morning wears on — lines to get through the metal detectors at the Municipal Airport and County Courthouse onerously long — all of it just a little bit aggravating, to say the least, making one feel like they're inside one enormous secret CIA detention center, recalling to someone's mind something he read about some guy from Argentina who testified that if we thought for one moment that *sitting hooded, all the time* is just a figure of speech, we should think again, that this was not the case because detainees were made to sit on the floor with nothing to lean against from the moment they got up at six in the morning until eight in the evening, when they went to bed, so that they spent fourteen hours a day in this position, and that when he said *without talking or moving*, he meant exactly that because they couldn't utter a *word*, or even turn their heads, for chrissake, and how, on one occasion, a companion ceased to be included on the interrogators' list and was forgotten, and how, after a full six months went by, they, his captors, only then realized what had happened because one of the guards thought it strange that the prisoner never wanted for anything and was always in the same condition, sitting there, hooded, without speaking or moving, for six months, awaiting death, prompting us to ask ourselves if we are in Argentina circa 1978 (we're obviously not), the contrasting perspective forcing us to take a breath, to put our heads down and push on, discovering

that all our work on this issue — on trying to see things from another point of view, as through the eyes of our wives, for instance — finally amounts to a dry pile of nothing much, some stupid, under-stuffed pelt of so-called porcupine, to take the example used earlier, or *worse*, except now everyone's just a little angrier and worn out for the effort (basically the mood, really, of the fall of mankind) because there's never any conclusion to be reached, just tiredness and anger, a place where even the simple questions don't receive an easy answer (whether the white cubes in the deli-bought pasta salad *are* cheese — probably, therefore, Swiss — or meat, meaning chicken) during some brutally silent meals, the TV set atop the dining room table droning on and on, often without commercial interruption, so when as darkness falls against the drapes, we often find ourselves imagining our server down at the DNR uncrated, growing hot, hot, hot with the buzz of commerce, so hot in fact that someone will probably need to install little cooling fans, until we wake as if in a dream, finding ourselves once again in our dark dining rooms, smack in the middle of an increasingly silent and suddenly sexless so-called marriage, wondering what the point of all this is, how it is that overnight we seem to have been reduced to these exhausted bodies, evidently good only for redirecting airflow lately, our eyes so dry and strained that it's difficult to decipher exactly what the 23 items advertised in the Z-tech three-person Bloodborne Pathogen/Bodily Fluid Spill Kit are, to say nothing of the ridiculous position paper Xeroxed and distributed by the Women's Alliance for Peace (re: an elaboration on the one-month celibacy so-called experiment, a warning shot over the bow, so to speak) explaining how the *Sutras* tell us that when we are established in continence, vigor is regained (in clear language, celibacy saves energy), and how in the name of loving and giving, the women apparently lose this energy and become mentally

and physically depleted (in other words sick and tired, a state of being prompting us to say welcome to *our* club), but clearly, we might respond, it's as plain as the nose on their faces, when you love somebody, you don't *stop* giving, that's the deal, a position in direct contradiction to their own, meaning that it is *precisely* because of our love that they, the women, don't know what to give, that love blinds us all (nice cliché there), making us greedy for more attachment — the very source of our pain and suffering — the name of our curse (we completely get this, that, for example, sometimes men and women even give one another venereal diseases, thereby spoiling the health of the one we love, and how giving someone the clap isn't giving someone a dozen roses, is in fact no gift at all, obviously), but in contrast, the argument of their manifesto continues, sexual fluid gives strength and stamina to the brain and nerves, and once abstinent (for one month and one month only), their minds, they predict, will be able to

focus without the distraction of their animal
instincts to attract a mate, to subdue a mate, to
enter into sexual congress with a mate, to
procreate, however domestic and *normal* these
activities might seem to be, their point here finally
arrived at (as the dwindling bullet points on the
Xerox indicate), that it's precisely because these
activities are so domestic and commonplace that
they are so dangerous, inasmuch as if they are
celibate for one month, they will perhaps
understand how much of their physical and mental
energies are expended in the execution of their
animal instincts — with the added benefit that
maybe you, meaning us, will take the opportunity
to think about our own behavior lately — for if
sexual energy *is* our life, if stored properly, it's
possible that we can distribute the energy and
focus it elsewhere, that possibly by observing
celibacy we might be able to preserve not just
physical energy alone but mental, moral,
intellectual and, ultimately, spiritual energy as

well, and consequently (possibly), as our sexual
energy is preserved it will get transformed into a
subtle energy called *ojas* (*ozone*, translated),
allowing us, perhaps, in the early morning before
sunrise to go out together and breathe the ozonic
wind, which it says here has a special vibration and
energy to it, the effect being lost once the sun's
rays come, and is apparently why the period
between four and six in the morning is called the
divine period, a very sacred time to meditate on
the ojas, those that will apparently make us glow
and transmit positive energy, and, just like
preserved honey becomes crystallized, it says, our
sexual fluids will be likewise transformed and
diffused, a sentiment, IT points out, that sure
sounds sweet, as in that it doesn't sound sweet at
all, that it just sounds *stupid*, an unnecessarily
hostile remark that must be taken with a grain of
salt, especially considering the strain IT has been
under lately with the impending adult
entertainment enterprise being placed, at least

initially, squarely on its shoulders, causing it to carry the nervous air of one whose order to join a bloody battle is imminent and is therefore requesting a short break before it begins, a long weekend, an afternoon off to get a tooth fixed, have a haircut, before the full force of the pressure bears down fully upon it, which, though reasonable requests all, are denied, leaving IT wondering aloud how it is that it's suddenly become the center of all this horseshit, when all it really wanted to do was study dolphins, every teenage girl's desire, sure, but put the school-girl aspect aside for a minute, IT explains, and throw in the fact that to get into information and technology in the first place you have to be pretty good in the basic sciences, including marine biology, then add in some more than decent grades in high school science in general, and what one's left with is the fact that there are probably twenty people on the whole planet who *actually study dolphins*, so up pops these internships at the Department of Inland

Fisheries whose facilities include a little room with a glass window cut below the embankment of the Upper Fork River, a cool and dark place (this room), the water lit behind the window, the only equipment needed being a hand-held counter so that every time a fish swims by it's counted, each and every fish, a task, IT says, that lends itself to daydreaming about life back on the Earth's surface with the game wardens among the trees (evidently what one misses most down there are terrestrial sounds, dry smells and sunlight), until it's discovered that there are maybe twenty game wardens in the *entire* State who actually warden game, and this number will continue to shrink unless some cost-saving measures can be found and implemented, like, right now (meaning back then, when it was initially employed by the DNR), like going paperless, for instance, a move that saves a small bundle for sure on expenditures like paper, but to do so requires an immediate web presence — office hours, driving directions,

application forms, basic stuff, local stuff —
requiring someone to actually *make* the web page,
an ability back in the day that precious few knew
how to do, and those who did were in serious
demand, so now the DNR pays for retraining
some of the would-be wardens, retooling them, as
it were, in said Information and Technologies, the
transition from one field to the other not as jarring
as one might think, because the name of the game
in biology — molecular, marine, mammal, what
have you — is, after all, pattern and distribution,
inasmuch as someone trained to study dolphins or
work as a game warden has to have a pretty good
eye for the larger forces at work in the ecosystem,
that it's exactly the same thing for web design, if
you think about it, meaning the distribution and
patterns that give a sense of the larger informational
order, indexing and cross-indexing and basic
alphabetization, as in *adorable, amateur, Asian, ass,
Bob Lerner*, to give an example of what IT's been
working on all morning, specifically how to

distribute seven hundred fifty units of *Bob Lerner's Guide to Animal Tracking in the American Midwest* in the first two quarters to begin to cover the cost of the dispersal of his information, so while the unit is discrete, the unit transacted into the broader marketplace takes in the larger system of commerce (it's at this level, IT points out, that we need you to *want* it, the *Guide*), despite the fact that informal surveys indicate that its challenge in creating a marketing push for the *Guide* is that it bores its reader shitless — an enormous challenge indeed — seeing the subject is of so little interest even to us, though undoubtedly it's of great interest to Bob Lerner and also the DNR, the latter of whom is willing to throw an unexpectedly large amount of cash (in the form of an anonymous, private donor, probably Bob Lerner himself, IT suspects) behind it in hopes that it both becomes a revenue source and stirs up historically low interest in our natural resources and the subsequent offices thereof, which is all hunky-dory, except that in a meeting Bob Lerner himself floats animal tracks on Yahoo's main page — as in animal tracks, follow them, to *Bob Lerner's Guide to Animal Tracking in the American Midwest* — a proposal, at least on the surface of it, that sounds good, except Bob Lerner hasn't the foggiest notion of what an invoice for a thousand hits on Yahoo looks like, because Bob Lerner is too busy tracking his fish right out of the water, reaffirming the notion held by IT that Bob Lerner doesn't know caribou crap from content, that even though Bob Lerner will undoubtedly have an opinion altogether different than the one expressed here, the fact remains that old Bob Lerner doesn't know bear shit from content, that while Bob Lerner might know that the ropey-dopey ends of a turd indicates a carnivore — there's a little factoid straight from the *Guide* — he doesn't know bobcat cakes about bringing in traffic, and besides, IT points out, Bob Lerner's the kind of guy who pays fifty bucks for a high-end haircut, then tells the barber exactly what he

wants, but if that's what Bob Lerner wants then he should be shelling out seven bucks at EconoCuts, or, better yet, just cut his own goddamned hair because, IT says, it really, really, really does *not* have time for this kind of shit anymore, because, like, work is really, really *busy*, it just doesn't stop, the stress caused by such considerations generally making it long for much simpler times — Clothes Folder at an all-night Laundromat, to name another historically held occupation, or the aforementioned Fish Tabulator below the banks of the Upper Fork — when everyone needing their clothes folded got their clothes folded, and when there was a fish that needed counting somebody was there to count it, or take the romantic allure of potato farming, including the planting of the potatoes, watering and weeding them, the helping them grow until harvest, when the potato farmer gathers them up and makes potato pie, boiled potatoes, potato bread, mashed potatoes and French fried potatoes, to name just a few of the delicious side dishes available to the potato farmer's family, assembled to eat at the great table set beneath the yawning shade of some big old trees, instead of this stuff, a memorandum of sorts emailed for dissemination to the IT Department, titled *Burqa Bitches*, subtitled *a modest proposal*, composed and circulated by someone proclaiming an active interest in R & D, and containing an argument for the development of an adult website based on the following summarized premises, that (1) several of us see a need to diversify beyond web hosting alone (again, a salient argument, but one not yet satisfactorily made), and (2) an inkling that a Mideast category would yield impressive numbers (i.e., traffic), based on a simple idea that follows the model of *school girls, teachers, secretaries, nuns*, meaning basic fantasy role play, mildly fetishistic, costumes, the burqa itself (its importance evidenced by the title), with its full closure, would make production bone-headedly easy as the director could put anyone in it so that

the model doesn't even need to be anything special
to look at, and we could shoot the whole thing in
a room at some Motel 6, or wherever, as long as
we had a burqa starring in something with a
(hopefully) more basic premise, with (hopefully)
more reasonably executed production values than,
well, an *airplane*, like something simply shot off
the shoulder, perhaps even with only one other
person in the cast, a missionary, or a tourist, or a
soldier who walks into the model's hovel, a pretty
trimmed down set, something as simple as a table
with a loaf of Wonder Bread on it, maybe a hookah
or some other little detail for the sake of
authenticity, but really, we're talking cinder block
walls, whatever, easy-peasy, a couch, a hovel into
which the actor walks, prompting the babe in the
burqa to perform that high-pitched tongue
clucking that you see on the TV news until the guy
grabs her, bends her over the couch, lifts her burqa
up from behind, and goes to town, either vaginally
or anally, which she resists at first, of course, but
then begins to appreciate so that screaming

becomes pleasurable moaning right up until the moment of the money shot, a million dollar money shot, it's argued, that takes place on her veiled face, roll credits, thus ending the most topically innovative proposals we've yet to encounter, probably the first of its kind, so that, we have to admit it, while a good number of us still remain reluctant to entertain a transition from web hosting to directing, the meager budget required for such a production, including not having to shell out for major talent, should perhaps persuade us that *Burqa Bitches* be entered for consideration, right up there alongside the Thumbtack's Stillman facility rehab on Strategic Planning's agenda, convening right after today's informal Bag Lunch Club, where our moderator, an HR Supervisor, who — neither directly involved in budgetary matters nor therefore in attendance at the preceding budgetary meeting, lucky skunk — finds us huddling around one of IT's laptops at the end of the conference table, causing a dirty smirk

to grouse beneath his mustache, setting him to loping around the conference table and, bending over our backs, asking what's up, fellas, to which we inform him that the real-time telemetry feed on KLM's website is tracking an aircraft in Netherlands airspace, a heading East/South Eastward at 570 miles per hour over Amersfoort, a distant Dutch city inspiring someone to remark that we shouldn't be fooled by those wooden shoes and loamy sunrises, because the Dutch remain the industry standard in just about every industry conceivable, eliciting the question as to whether or not our newly emergent expert on international business affairs meant *gloomy*, not *loamy* (nice content, loamy, IT adds), itself garnering a response to the effect that *gloamy* is a loamy sunrise in reverse, a peaty sunset (look, someone points out the window now, it's really snowing, and the response, it was supposed to snow), a conversationally parenthetical interjection that brings the conversation to the subject of snow itself, how it's snowing in Netherlands' airspace, although apparently not enough to disrupt air traffic, a phenomena not without precedence, someone adds, as it's *always* snowing somewhere in Netherlands' airspace, and, presumably by way of contrast, someone adds that India has become an international warm weather destination, not just a warm weather city, but a warm weather *country*, so that KLM advertises four flights to India daily from Chicago's O'Hare Airport, and that's just one airport, one airline (someone wonders aloud here just how many rupees make a dollar), flying direct to Mumbai, where it's presently 35 degrees Celsius, speaking of which, Mumbai, someone says, the impulse toward independence is understandable enough, but it's still difficult not to have romantic notions associated with olden times, however unfounded these may be, insofar as it's hard to feel less than ambivalent over the loss of the city of Bombay, for example, as opposed to Baghdad, on the other hand, because given the

ambiguous future of Baghdad, well, someone else
can have Baghdad, we'll take Bombay, or the
Spanish capital of Madrid, as spoken by astronauts
in post-launch communications, speaking of
romantic, flights to Madrid filled to capacity after
the astronauts spoke it (Madrid, *Madrid*), a fact
that compels the HR moderator (his smirk having
disappeared) to indicate that it might be useful to
log-off for a moment, as it were, and focus our
emotional intelligence on a discussion about crisis
intervention, stressing that while no mandatory
evals and training for municipal employees is yet
slated, his mandate here is to show us ways to
preemptively avoid emotional crises that might
hamper our abilities to effectively intervene,
should such an intervention, god forbid, be
required, through practicing such techniques as
unconditional focus, or identifying the warning
signs of PTSD (the *i*'s alone, we notice in the index
of the handout he begins distributing, runs the
gamut from *incontinence* to *irritability*), with the

former, unconditional focus, both accessible and exercisable by doing a little assignment, he says, involving the drawing of a picture of a loved one, a spouse or significant other, on the pages of yellow legal pads he also distributes along with stubby little pencils (feels unnervingly like a test, someone quips), until after ten or fifteen minutes of this he asks us to stop and calls on one of us to hold up his drawing, a poorly executed triangle because, its maker confesses, he's not what one would call a terrific artist (one's artistic ability isn't the point here, the HR moderator emphasizes), and now we're asked to come together as a group and analyze it, to unconditionally focus on it in order to objectively validate the feelings, the moderator says, the artist may have drawn into it, so we begin, hesitantly at first, repeating the obvious, that it's indeed a picture, albeit one requiring an uncommon amount of interpretation, that is, if the picture is supposed to be the artist's wife in the first place (yes, it *is* supposed to be his wife,

it's affirmed), wearing a dress — the triangle is supposed to be a dress, the little circle above it, her head — titled by the artist as *The Wife, number two pencil on lined paper*, featuring a squiggly, star-like object on her shoulder, maybe a bug, an octopus rather, the artist interjects, forcing certain subsidiary questions surrounding, for example, what his wife is doing in what looks to be mountains, carrying an octopus and wearing a dress, to which our artist responds that if we look closer, we'll discover that it's a seafloor, actually, a rift valley inside an unnamed mid-ocean mountain range, where she, his wife, is giving herself freely to the octopus, and that it's very quiet down here except for the mechanical suck and intermittent burping of a scuba regulator, a description, taken as a whole, we agree is very conceptual, and we wonder what it means, exactly, that the artist himself is nowhere to be found in the picture, when someone who apparently has some expertise in photography suggests that the wife is the only subject in the picture because, as a rule, he who *takes* the picture is never *in* the picture, and yet, someone presses, it's a drawing, not a photograph, an indisputable point, but for the fact, comes the reply, that he who *makes* the picture is never in the picture, and that we're also disregarding another fact involving the notion that there is the *suggestion* of the picture maker, hence the suck and burping of the regulator, an altogether excellent point, it's affirmed, drawing our attention to the contrasting detail that she's not wearing one, the wife, a regulator, evidently because she doesn't have to, the artist explains, because she can't be bothered with such so-called mortal coils the rest of us must endure — health insurance premiums or regular, preferably monthly deposits into a 401K account to help feed her when she's too geriatric to fend entirely for herself — down there in her underwater valley (the fact that she's underwater explains the squiggly lines, but we still aren't exactly sure why

we're underwater to begin with), where the wife embraces the octopus and the octopus embraces the wife under the ocean, as the ocean itself, the artist *feels*, represents her subconscious, an unnameable ocean because it remains a previously undiscovered topographical feature of her own precious self who is just batty-ass *crazy* for that goddamned octopus, its eight arms symbolizing the eight limbs of yoga (most often depicted as a tree, the artists adds, in case we didn't know), three of which are looped around her shoulder, three looped around her thighs, while one follows the crease of her buttocks — it's impossible to see this from the angle she's represented, we're told — hooks around her perineum, flicking at her navel, and the last one, the eighth limb, runs up the back of her neck, drapes over the crown of her head, dangles here between her eyes in a composition that, artistic ability aside, suggests to us how completely yoga has taken hold of the women while, from our vantage point, we're left

suspended here, left to look on helplessly while
our air tanks go empty, an image of a certain
depth, we agree, constructed there on the ocean
floor, where below seven atmospheres it's not the
bends but the pressure that'll kill a scuba diver, a
nautical line of inquiry of surprising interest to a
large number of us that's cut short by the HR
moderator, who suggests that we shift gears here
and maybe just kick back and shoot the breeze,
have a powwow *mano a mano*, a moment to talk
about how we're all doing today, how we're
feeling, what — leaving aside briefly the terrible
September 11 attacks and corresponding work
issues (these anxieties, he says, are already pretty
well identified) — our concerns are our fears, the
more so-called holistic fear of the uncertain future
our children will be born into, for example, a
world that increasingly looks like a public toilet,
or the more localized fears of drive-by shooters
cruising our front porches, pedophiles stalking
our sidewalks, Radon gasses pooling in the

basement, drunk drivers on the street, arsenic in the tap water, lead in the paint, low-flying aircraft, how they make everyone nervous, especially since they've rotated the flight patterns at the Municipal Airport again and the brunt of descending traffic flies right over the middle of town, a low cloud ceiling rolling in at dusk — thick and gray, reflecting rather than absorbing the lights from the city — adding to the spookiness as the airplanes seem to pop out of it, the weather, all at once, and once they appear, they fly just below it, the sound of their engines echoing off of it as they fly low and slow toward the airport, so that at night we have to close the blinds and draw the curtains in order to block out the chromium leer of their landing lights, adding yet another disturbance to already restless nights, full of these fears and the fear mixed with the inevitable, all pervasive guilt born from the nagging memories of the various injuries and potentially life-ending accidents that many of our children have already lived through, a type of general conversation, our moderator interjects, that we can only have from the vantage point of brute strength, of having *successfully fulfilled* our parental obligations thus far, full in our dominion over the dangers hunting our children down, like a potentially life-threatening catastrophe, one of the younger fathers now recounts, that involved his ascending the stairs, his baby in one arm and a two liter bottle of Diet Coke in the other, and how he slipped, all of it happening in a split second of a split second, and how he dropped the soda bottle and caught his baby by the leg midair just before its head was going to hit the concrete step of the stoop, an anecdote prompting a general discussion about our fears of dropping babies — particularly those of us who are not so-young fathers, who are concerned that age might impinge on reaction time, how age dulls the instincts so therefore the baby might be dropped — a more or less universal concern among us because so many of the women

are in fact having babies that we've struck up an informal agreement with our local Border's franchise owner to buy baby shower gifts in bulk (thus securing a bulk discount), a gross of *Pat the Bunny* books, that calming, sweet little story evoking a lot of good and simple memories among us when we're reintroduced to Paul and Judy, and told they can do lots of things, and we can do lots of things, too, in this beloved classic, wherein Paul and Judy play peek-a-boo, smell flowers, look in the mirror, feel Daddy's scratchy face, and, of course, pat the bunny, amounting to eight activities in this timeless favorite sure to fascinate the little ones, as it has for over sixty years, during which time, the back of the book tells us, Dorothy Kunhardt's *Pat the Bunny* has sold over six million copies and is one of the bestselling children's books of all time, all and all an absolutely fair and square deal, meaning she's *earned* it, as evidenced by the fact that we have a hard time putting the book down, such is its ability to recall that ephemeral state of innocence, its memory replaced now by a printed copy on an email that was sent to IT's inbox overnight, an email that IT meant to give to HR earlier, but, you know, *spaced* on it, but it's a real piece of work, IT says, that couldn't be farther down the vibe-o-meter from what we're discussing, as if some nutjob was reading *Pat the Bunny* right before writing it and set out to make, for whatever trippy reason, its opposite, the sender's address unknown to us, without subject line, the content revealing that its writer has been watching the women talking in low whispers at the park, how they giggle and sigh as if they're pleasuring (his word) themselves in front of him, their spoken words like little buzzing rabbit vibrators in his ears, and how when one of the women speaks, the one spoken to looks at her mouth, and then into her eyes, and back to the mouth again, and that it's *too much*, the way their hind-ends hang from the swings, as if they were about to perform the Bengalese Basket Fuck, or

how they teeter-totter with their legs opened
wide, their hands stuffed into their open pusses
[*sic*], going up and down, up and down, teeter-
tottering, teeter-tottering, that it's all just too
goddamned much how they hang from the monkey
bars, as if they were holding on to the heated towel
rod in the tub surround, their heads thrown back,
stretching, their hair hanging off their heads in
big, pull-able bunches, or how they lie idly in the
blue polymer well of the SuperSlide, staring up
into the clear blue sky with their wet mouths agape
so that the author of the insidious email just wants
to step onto the scene and fuck them all, if only he
could remove the children from the area ☹ (his
so-called punctuation), an alarming end to an
alarming message, unavoidably indicating that
there appears to be a stalker amongst us, that
obviously someone's jumping off the deep end, a
gesture obviously not to be taken lightly, the HR
moderator announces, a clear case for the proper
authorities — the police, obviously — who will

conduct their investigation, analyze the language
of the message and undoubtedly determine what's
already apparent to us, arriving at the inescapable
conclusion that the details are too eerily intimate
to come from an outside source and should not
therefore be considered a hoax, prompting
interviews to be conducted, the field of suspects
narrowed down to those of us with heated towel
racks installed in the tub surrounds of our homes
(informal questioning reveals that this is an
unusually common feature, alas), and meanwhile
we'll wait for another email, because that's all we
can do in the interim between the one message
and the next, wait, and listen and watch, remaining
open and attentive to verbal and non-verbal cues
alike, including aversive glances around the
conference room, general lack of eye contact
altogether, the flash of a sneaky grin, sudden
shifting, a telltale twitch inside a suspicious silence
broken only by the alternating percolation of
digestive acids and the growl of someone's empty

stomach, when finally, thankfully, someone says that, speaking of the women, we haven't heard how thing's went at marriage counseling yesterday, where the topics determined prior to the session were to include (1) equitability, (2) silence and (3) anger, prompting our session representative to first sigh a sigh that sounds suspiciously like relief, then ask for a moment to recollect his thoughts, revealing after several seconds that, with regard to our first issue — equitability — the marriage counselor advised us to close our eyes and think of our marriage as a field of dirt filled with many holes so that here we all are, the women and us, standing in the bottom of our respective holes dug with our respective shovels, all of us digging like our lives depend upon it, and while we're throwing shovels of dirt shovelful by shovelful into their holes, they, the women, are trying to dig their own holes, too, but first they must shovel out the dirt that we're throwing into their holes, which they do, making an ever-growing pile at the side of their holes in a ratio that seems a little skewed, someone points out, because they're surely throwing dirt into our holes, too, a discrepancy that our representative noticed as well and pointed out to the marriage counselor who asked for the liberty to summarize the argument on our behalf, saying that, in our view, if the counselor had it right, we're in our hole throwing dirt into their hole, and they're in their hole, throwing dirt into our hole, ergo, no one is able to satisfactorily dig their own holes, a summation that we agree sounds pretty right, although the marriage counselor apparently does not, deeming it wrong without even seeming to think about it, adding that given the statistical ratio of dirt displacement over time by gender, we're putting more dirt into their hole than they're able to put into our hole, a ratio, furthermore, indicative of our blind selfishness on the matter (yikes), so now, with regard to the second topic (silence), the marriage counselor apparently did agree that the women's use of the

so-called silent treatment — we mean *real* silence, not the normal kind wherein the refrigerator hums, the heat kicks in after a mechanical preamble, the foundation of the house adjusts to subtle variances in barometric pressure, wind chimes, snow blowers, aircraft, something's beeping, the next door neighbor threatening to beat his dog to death, falling asleep with the television on, the maddening tune whistled by the obsessive whistlers among us — sure does put a damper on communication, that if we're accused of either emotional or physical cheating, for instance (at cards, on the taxes, of having an extramarital affair, of course), and the accuser takes a vow of silence on the matter right after the accusation is made, there's certain to be an emergent problem here because, obviously, it's impossible to defend oneself against silent judgment, accusations (e.g., the absurd position that we're put in) likened now to getting a parking ticket in the mail and then having to prove that the car wasn't parked on 1st and Strawberry way the hell over there in Richmond, Virginia, on October 13th, a possibility that fails to account for the fact that we live half a country away, or whatever, so fine, okay, now *prove* it, such instances leading us to situations that sound a lot like an Inflatabed expiring on the living room floor, the floorboards creaking in the bedroom above where one's spouse has been sleeping alone, a hot pot of oatmeal bubbling on the stove, a kettle about to whistle, the sound of words to the answer of the age-old question regarding whether or not one is having an affair, plus unavoidable confrontations involving such stupid things as an empty pudding cup balancing on the summit of garbage accumulating above the rim of the trashcan in the summer kitchen, a trail of chocolate pudding that begins there, the intermittent pudding footprints leading into the kitchen, ending beneath the culprit's left hunting sock, such a stupid chain of events, but a clear trail to be followed to a clear subject for

confrontation nevertheless, when instead what
one wants to really know is whether or not the
other spouse is fucking someone else, or is even
thinking about fucking someone else, by which we
mean that it isn't bad enough already that we've a
full-blown Jihad on our hands and that, given the
chance, half the Arab world wants to cut the head
off our President and use it to defile our women
and our children, but now there's *this* craziness, a
situation that even the marriage counselor couldn't
suggest an adequate response to, in part because
our session was nearly over, so that finally, with
regard to the last topic — anger issues — we
apparently ran completely out of time, an
unfortunate development to be sure as there are
many anger issues, including their — the women's
— tendency toward physical abuse, specifically
their propensity to physically lash out in our
bedrooms, to give one example, and in the upstairs
hallways (also reportedly in the basement once),
and yet, if what's important here is not *where* these

incidents occurred but where on the body the abuse *landed*, then we should be looking on the arms, mostly, occasionally on the chest, a distinction that matters (between where they occurred and where on the body the occurrence took place), someone emphasizes, because, at least in American jurisprudence, these distinctions are the difference between homicide and manslaughter, as in one's intent to do harm, the distinction itself necessitating a follow-up question involving the motivation to do harm in the first place, how we're all angry sometimes, how we're all of us are haunted by our pasts — a cliché, sure, but a statement that doesn't lose its *oomph* by being so — a generalization that unfortunately falls way short of being useful in distinguishing the physically violent from the physically nonviolent, the very crux of the issue here, meaning what, exactly, happened in the violent women's pasts that resulted in the instantaneous use of force, a question that is fundamentally unanswerable, we

resolve, given their individual experiences, until someone offers up the fact that it's commonly known that one in four girls is molested before her eighteenth birthday, a really appalling statistic that we might keep in mind the next time we're in a room with four or more women, with or without the wife, someone adds, himself therefore asked point-blank if his own wife has ever been molested, soliciting the response that if we get five women in a room, one has been molested, statistically speaking, which is kind of the point here, he says and, when pressed again whether his wife has ever been molested, the answer comes in the form of a soft negative (allowing thus for possibility), a negative further qualified by the observation that there seems to be something back there (history), the way they retreat into themselves sometimes, a depression, maybe, pretty gloomy, maybe depression, but if it's not a depression, precisely, it's maybe anxiety, although maybe something more sedate and profound than anxiety, something

closer to extended bouts of sulking, a description
that's getting close to sounding like a professional
diagnosis, it's pointed out, causing some uneasiness
among us, diagnostically speaking, particularly as
sulking is obviously a descriptor, not a clinical
category — meanwhile someone wonders aloud
here where the Mayor is, what could be keeping
him so long — though we've often found ourselves
standing before it, the sulk, in baffled silence,
watching the water in the Britta water pitcher
filter, but anyway, interrupts our delegate to the
marriage counseling, as for the present, between
now and the next session we're supposed to
continue to work at projecting our feelings
outwards, making *exceedingly deliberate attempts*
(the counselor's wishes) at projecting our feelings
outward, working to give voice to our emotions at
all times in *all environments*, such that the fluffy
flakes falling on the green dumpsters outside look
to us like volcano ash, suggesting, someone
remarks, that our world, this world, feels as

though it's being burned to ashes — that this is the whole significance of the word *ash* here — likewise the remark that the gurgling of the dehumidifier sounds like the death rattle of someone with emphysema, or that the wheezing of the radiators sounds like someone dying of congestive heart failure, or the observation that the old, off-white colored walls of the conference room reminds one of mushrooms (obviously connoting burial and dampness), or that the fabric on all the crappy furniture in the reception area down the hall looks like margarine, emblematic of both its shabby greasiness and the connotation of the environment's heart-clogging properties, a line of inquiry thankfully halted here by the arrival (finally) of the Mayor who sits down at the conference table, drops his load of a half-dozen manila file folders, unbuttons the cuffs of his shirt and rolls his sleeves to the forearms, meanwhile looking into each of the faces before him, telling us that whoever is pulling this shit — here he's pointing to a copy of

the obscene email in front of the HR Director —
whoever's writing this crap on company time on
company computers and sending it over company
email better knock it off like right now, his last
word, his *now* given the force of a few more
decibels, and while we're here talking about doing
a little ass-kicking, the Mayor continues, he wants
to know when it is that we'll be able to expand
storage at the Blood Bank, when it is that he's
going to see another subterfuge to spin all that
surplus blood down, how it is that we haven't
gotten off the pot yet and, strictly between us, put
some hardcore fisting action on his monitor like
immediately, like yesterday, because, he's telling
us, he wants to see a spanking tomorrow *ante
meridiem*, and he wants to get *paid* for watching
that spanking in order to get the old blood flowing
in the Blood Bank, so, he says, he's serious, just
slap some tits and ass up and get on with it, to
which IT repeats the Mayor's directive, parroting
the phrase *just slap some tits and ass up*, adding *as if*,

explaining that it's not that easy, that if we want
traffic it has to be something more, something the
consumer hasn't seen yet in order to secure our
market share, because otherwise why bother,
seeing as the ether is already writhing with base
fantasies, with blunt nakedness and full exposure
made possible by only the most cutting-edge
cinematic technologies (plus, IT reminds us, we
don't even have the stupid new server yet), a
calmly delivered rationale that sets the Mayor off
in a tirade of shouted prerogatives, including clit
rings, cock rings, nipple rings, until, as if hearing
himself in the echo, he becomes quiet, lifts his
hands from the table and tells us to listen up, that
he's sorry, that he doesn't have to explain the
pressure he's been under lately, that he hasn't been
sleeping well, that, to be honest, he's been
suffering lately from what he summarizes as some
badass dreams involving regional atmospheric
scientists interrupting normal weather reporting
with brightly lit digital maps, maps our local

forecasters interpret for him, the Mayor, demanding that he and his constituency (us) prepare for what they describe as a monumental event, a nightmare scenario, really, a knuckle ball thrown by nature that can't be ducked (that's why they call it nature, the forecasters remind him), meaning, the Mayor says, Christ almighty does it ever *snow* in his dream, an official snow *event* starting in his dream on a Wednesday night around eight, a snow the forecasters say that they are one hundred percent certain is going to be very bad, that there's no way to really prepare for how bad it's going to be, and the Mayor believes it, for already when he looks out the window in his dream all he sees is white, despite its being night — it's not dark, just *white* outside — such is the volume of snow falling in his dream, so much snow in fact falling in such a short time that the salt trucks can't hardly get out of the garages to get out in front of it, and the one or two that do are stranded, the salt truck drivers struck dumb and

giddy by the fact, as suggested by the timber of their voices broadcast over emergency radio (the Mayor's manning a radio in the dream) — *no go*, he can hear them giggle, we're *stuck* — a phrase coming from his salt truckers that he's never dreamed of hearing, so that when the phone calls start pouring in for Emergency Services, there's nothing he can do but communicate the abysmal reality — the ambulances are stuck in the ambulance bays, the police and firemen are stuck at their stations — and even when he receives a call from his wife (in the dream they have already left for India, and now he is already dreaming of their return) informing him that they are packing their bags at the ashram, preparing to come home, he has to tell even them to hang tight, because we're getting *unbelievable* amounts of snow, a good fifteen feet in less than twelve hours in his dream, averaging thirteen and one-eighth inch per hour, more or less, the weight of it already beginning to snap tree limbs two hours after it starts so that there would be a complete communication and power blackout, except for the fortunate fact that our power and telephone lines are bundled with the cable underground thanks to some good, solid municipal planning back when, but still, the telephone system is quickly overwhelmed, EMS is offline, the cops can't come and thankfully there's no fires in his dream because the fire trucks are useless, even in chains, inasmuch as Government, at least what's left of it, is forced to operate on snowmobiles commandeered from the John Deere Co-op, taken outright with no dickering over price as permissible through our Emergency Authority Articles, so that by the time the Mayor and his posse of First Responders (many of whom are in this very room, he says) are able to get out and assess the situation at the break of day, the snow is over the eaves of the houses, smoking tree stumps in the faint morning light upon closer inspection found to be chimneys, the houses buried in a snow that fell for twelve hours straight,

now suddenly stopped, leaving a level field of
white where the town once stood, now gone, a
white plain except for those buildings above two
stories, which are not many, causing us in the
Mayor's dream to get into Municipal Hall through
an unlocked window on the second floor, making
our way downstairs to the DNR Annex, where
the snow is pressed against the smoked glass
windows, making the Mayor feel like he's entering
a quite tomb (evidently not a phone is ringing for
the moment, a fact that just isn't possible in so-
called reality), prompting him to set up a situation
room on the upper floors where we can make a
quick accounting of our assets, arriving at the fact
that we're in pretty sorry shape in the Mayor's
dream, except that one of us comes up with the
inspired idea that all of us should assemble in the
conference hall where we've a video camera for
our live cable feed on the Community Access
station, a camera we focus upon the Mayor, who
announces the obvious, that we have a situation

here with all the snow, but that we are on top of it, that everyone is undoubtedly already aware that their phones aren't working properly, but that this is a result of the system being overwhelmed so it's crucial, the Mayor says, that the phones are not used except to report a *true* emergency, by which he means he understands that we're worried about whether or not Grandma has enough medication, or if the kids stranded at the sleepover are safe, but we need to keep these lines clear for true emergencies, life and death, so that if Grandma doesn't actually have her medication, she can get a hold of us and we'll get Grandma's medication to her, that this is the best we can do at present, considering the circumstances, made immeasurably better by the idea one of his aids whispers in his ear while on-air, how they could power-up the unused server (obviously in his dream, the requisition order is finally fulfilled, and the CP 750 Whisper awaits us) downstairs in the DNR Annex to host a so-called community

bulletin board, where neighbors could get in touch with neighbors, where family members could communicate with family members, where we could get a sense of the condition of the community, a terrific idea that the Mayor immediately communicates live to our citizens, turning to us (lurking somewhere off camera) and ordering us to execute it, the idea, and we do, getting the server networked and up and running in a few hours, dream-time, the Mayor broadcasting the fact on Community Access that everyone with a computer should post their whereabouts and general condition at the following web address, the whole system seeming to work instantly, as messages start coming in right off the bat — *safe and sound, no worse for wear and tear, buried alive but doing alright* — and now recipes begin to appear, stuff the Mayor wouldn't think of, tuna fish pie with Ritz Cracker crust, stuff like that, together with advice on how to knock the cabin fever out of the little rug rats, but more importantly in the dream we were finding a way to prioritize search and rescue to those street addresses we haven't heard from, marking these locations with big X's on a zoning map, the upshot being that we made it through the crises with zero loss of life — we were now tested and we made it through okay — a fact remarked upon by the President himself, who, flying overhead in Air Force One, designates us a disaster area, and with that, the money starts pouring in, our budget crises finally over, the snow melting with the aid of an unseasonably warm and steady sun, certainly helping with snow removal in the dream, but, considering the sheer amount of snowmelt, the storm sewers are becoming quickly overwhelmed so that flooding is a major concern as we watch the water rise and rise, until the Mayor announces that what we really need to do is stop watching that goddamned water and get our hands on some shallow-hulled watercraft instead, compelling someone to remark that we never had temperatures this high at this

time of the year when we were kids, prompting
the Mayor to call it what it is, global warming, a
damned catastrophe, he says gravely, telling us
this is when he wakes up, looking searchingly back
up into our faces, drumming his fingers on the
conference table, his shirt sleeves a corrugated,
wrinkled mess of cotton/polyester tubing, his
limp cuffs now dangling over his wrists, a gloomy
silence coming over him, making some of us fidget
and cough, until the Mayor, sensing our unease,
opens the topmost file folder beneath his hands
and withdraws a June 1999 copy of *Barely Legal*, its
gaudy cover (a brunette with an overbite dressed
in a school uniform, her legs spread toward the
reader, just a little peek of her white panties under
her kilt) and slippery pages already a relic from
what seems to us an unknowable past, which the
Mayor now rolls into a baton and starts pounding
the table with, saying this is what he's talking
about, that if these jokers could get their act
together back in the dark ages, it behooves him to

wonder why the hell can't we, he says, letting the
magazine fall on the table where it breaks open to
an advertisement for Trojan condoms, soliciting
from us a contemplative silence, a silence that
again stretches out for an uncomfortably long time
until someone breaks it with a question, a
whimsical, wistful question that serves to lighten
the mood, asking if there's anything more erotic
than having someone say your name while sucking
you off, its bizarre brazenness immediately serving
to brighten the atmosphere made gloomy both by
the Mayor's dream and the obvious frustrations of
his predicament, so that we are all grateful for the
Mayor's chuckle here, and his suspicions that the
question's framer has a somewhat satisfying sex
life, but probably pretty short-lived and infrequent
— *abrupt*, in a word, comes the response — and
so the conversation turns to the mouth, the true
orifice of waste, someone says, said Sophocles, or
somebody like him, but still, take the basic mouth,
the lower lip, wow, the word *lips* sounding, the

Mayor interrupts, like someone waxing nostalgic
about good old American middle-aged oral sex,
adding that Camembert softens nicely with age
and also takes on a nutty, mellow flavor,
recommended by *Gourmet*, but, someone adds,
consider on the other hand the concept of low-
level dirty talk, nothing hostile, but dirty, a point
wholly disregarded as the conversation continues
to explore the issue-as-tabled, what the Mayor
now calls the good old American middle-aged
blow job, or oral sex altogether, because,
depending on one's point of view, either the
clitoris is a very small penis, or the penis is a very
large clitoris, a conclusion, however uncomfortable,
that points to the fact that we are all of us one, in
this sense, since oral sex is arguably of equal
interest to men and women alike, fetish or not, so
now that we've got that straight, the Mayor says,
as interesting as this little detour is, he wants to
hear some ideas right now that we can actually
work with, *anything*, people, someone help him out

here, he veritably pleads, until someone finally shouts out the phrase *cum shot*, then elaborates how it'd be a perfect name for our website — *Cum Shot* — the name speaking directly to the center of the business plan, like calling a business that sells containers *Containers and Things*, because, along with containers, Containers and Things does, in fact, sell a few things other than containers to their consumer base (folks in need of containers), bringing us to the question of who our consumer base would be — invariably someone looking for porn, yes, but who, exactly, is he, is the question — to which the person who proposed the name *Cum Shot* in the first place says, *exactly*, who he is, meaning, let someone else figure out the mean average of female desire, that we're *men* and should be marketing *toward* men, that we could create a boutique of sorts, wherein the cum shot reined supreme, and that we could take the principal strategy of the cum shot itself and apply it to the spectrum of our consumer's desires, implying, in

other words, that we shouldn't give a diddly shit about context but instead should just get in and out, giving them the thing in itself, not a single frame more, and that we could expand this to all sorts of content — a one-stop-shopping experience, as it were — including demolition footage of stadiums, high-speed watercraft caught at the moment of disintegration, office buildings imploding upon detonation, high-speed auto accidents, munitions dumps aflame, bombs destroying their targets, fireworks factories going up in fireworks, flood waters claiming summer homes, avalanches, various sports injuries at the very moment the injury takes place, hurricane force winds ripping off roofs, plane crashes, bomb tests, volcanoes, various folks under fire, monster smoke plumes, various folks on fire, tornadoes tearing into barns, shit in its most abbreviated form, not a second outside the frame of the actual event, not one single frame more, and, of course, various sexual organs caught at the moment of climax, the simplicity of the idea being so impressive that it's met with complete silence, our minds overcome with its power, striking us with the fact that what we've just possibly heard is the clear plan upon which to build an entertainment *empire*, a place where all of a man's entertainment needs are met, offered to him in a perfectly tailored, consolidated, almost primitive format that speaks to his most base consumer needs, so that suddenly even the Peterbuilt Triple-Axle Toxic Spill Abatement Vehicle seems within reach, until someone brings up the trifling little problem of copyright infringement, pretty much killing the dream as quickly as it appeared, this almost, nearly perfect idea, the Mayor says, that represents the out-of-the-box thinking that might well get us through this mess, a kind of out-of-the-boxiness he'd like to spend the day brainstorming here, but he's got to make his appearance at the Strategic Planning meeting for a little hand-on-hand holding action with the Director of Parks and Recreation,

who's supposed to let the hammer drop on
Thumbtack and her bitching about those floors, a
problem he could give a flat fuck about, but the
Director's going to break the news to her, that
whatever it is, it's a flat-out *no*, and we all know
how crazy she and that goddamned club of hers
are, and he means absolutely nutso stubborn, so
he's really got to scoot, but excellent, he says as he
gets up from the table, telling us to keep up the
good work as he heads for the door and then is
gone, leaving us to our own initiative, with IT
picking up the ball by announcing that it's funny,
speaking of dreams, there's this one about coming
home from work, opening the toilet lid to take a
leak and finding a turd in there — specifically, a
large, reddish-black turd, cylindrical and ropey
with tapered ends, what's called, à la Bob Lerner,
nipple-dimple ends, characteristic of a carnivore
— but the problem is that the wife, she's a
vegetarian, an *herbivore*, so what's one supposed to
do, except maybe turn from the toilet and ask the

wife directly if she had any visitors recently, any at all, to which she says no, of course, leaving the entire IT Department to begin the day mulling over the haunting question of what's more troubling, someone coming to the house to play a little slap and tickle with one's wife, or his (the interloper) taking a dump in the bathroom afterwards, but anyway, the dream aside, IT announces that it's about to deliver the graphical user interface even as we speak, compelling somebody to point out that, speaking of graphical user interfaces, the thing about jargon is that it's exclusionary, an interesting phenomena, actually, when one considers how communist countries rely so much on jargon — Brother Number One, Brother Number Two, and so on — meaning, IT responds, some foundational code for our website is complete, as is the invoice for its completion (side comment: there was probably a Sister Number One in the Khmer Rouge, because those were some real badasses, those Khmer Rouge),

forcing IT to attempt further clarification by
stating that the code is complete, the content
expected, thus provoking another side comment
about technology, a question about where the silly
switch is on that thing (technology, in general, but
more specifically an IBM Secretary being pointed
at, sitting under a plastic cover on a cabinet in the
corner), clearly intended to drive home the fact
that, for most of us, tech stuff might as well be
voodoo, like talking to most of us about what
seems intuitive to the IT Department is like taking
our Subarus to a loom for tune-ups (meanwhile,
IT is still trying to make its point here, that
technology and content, they're two different
things) or having a root canal performed by a hair
colorist (code is code, content is content,
information is inform-ation, or in-forming-ation,
minus the -ation part), to which someone adds
that, speaking of colorists, what's with that broad
suing her hair stylist for twenty-eight million
dollars, speaking of bad hair days, compelling IT

to announce that he'll explain it just one more
time for the benefit of the uber-tardos among us,
that content is a whole universe of content itself,
that the real deal about content is that, as soon as
it finds a hole in the dike one's trying to build
around oneself, *dude, everything* pours through it,
even though most of us don't even care about the
form of content in the first place, but instead we're
just trying to navigate through the space, trying to
pass through as fast as we can hustle on our way to
something else, dragging our own debris trail of
content as we go, so the problem here is trying to
get somebody to slow down and stay and *see* — it's
a lot easier said than done — the magic word here
being *affordance*, a word that IT likens to an infant
sitting in the center of a rifled-through *Tribune*,
the Sunday edition, an image of the infant stunned
beyond crying, really stunned, IT means *crying,*
because, being a baby, it can't begin to comprehend
the issue of affordance, the qualities of the physical
world that suggest the *possibility* of interaction

relative to the ability of an actor to interact,
meaning whether or not the technology user
perceives that clicking on the object is a meaningful,
useful action, with a known outcome, as in the
question of whether or not this here chair is a nice
place to sit, itself a classical, deeply complicated
affordance question, including all the implications
of the environmental, cultural, instinctual issues
that shape the mental model of our understanding
and expectations when we interact with, in this
case, a chair, but in the end — and this is to our
great advantage, IT says, you bunch of babies —
we have learned to click on underlined things
automatically, which is a *super-huge* step, IT says,
surveying the faces in the room, undoubtedly
noticing our blank stares, the fact that we're
completely lost, an acknowledgment announced
with one loud hand clap, an audible end-
punctuation to all the abstractions, and then a
transition in the form of the phrase, *check this out*,
followed by an introduction to a yoga class,

described as a room full of athletic babes in tights, when in walks this guy who unrolls his sticky mat in the center of them, faces teacher who's hot, hot, *hot*, calling everyone's attention to the middle of the room, where she's going to demonstrate a new *position*, and she most definitely does, then hot yoga action ensues, meaning like a ten-on-one, all shot through the spy camera placed in the dude's (therefore our) eyeglasses, allowing us to see — if we can go back to the beginning here — hot teacher walking toward us, telling us to stand up, so we stand up, to get into the Triangle pose (nice allusion to a threesome), grabs us by the ass and elbow, bends us over, blathers some technical detail, has us stand up again, revealing that we've got a boner, as seen through his (our) eyes, looking down at the *massive* bulge in our shorts, our hand flitting around trying to hide it, a quick pan here around the group of women surrounding us, apparently trying to detect if they've already noticed our huge hard-on, which they notice, all

right, because they're all clearly *staring* at the package, smiling dirtily, licking their lips, until the teacher says *oh my*, and proceeds to pull down our shorts, while the yoga students close in like a pack of animals on a fresh kill, prompting a hand to shoot up here, followed by a question about the rationale for the spy cam to be mounted in the glasses, causing IT to remind us of the Trends Analysis discussed in the morning meeting, that we're following the money, but still, the initial framer says, the question can be fairly asked anyway, that if we didn't know we were going to pop a rod and be embroiled in a hot yoga sex free-for-all, why is it that we're walking around with a hidden camera on our head, a faulty summation to begin with, someone intercedes, because the camera is hidden *in* our glasses, that clearly we're just a guy who walks around with a hidden camera in his glasses, just in case, that's all, we mean, if we weren't walking around with a camera hidden in our glasses, imagine what we'd *miss*, the word hanging in the air, taking on volume — miss, misses, missed, missing, Ms., Mrs. — recalling to mind the Mayor and his (the Parks and Recreation Director, rather, with the Mayor at his side) meeting so that we begin wondering aloud how it might be going between him and Thumbtack, each of us privately running through the various scenarios that might result from it, the whole stupid floor issue, yes, but, we wonder, if the subject of the India trip (and prohibition thereof) is going to come up, too, and the women's staying so that everything up to this point remains relatively unchanged, or their actual leaving, actually catching some outbound flight to India, a scheduled departure late at night or at the crack of dawn, regardless, so by the time *Good Morning America* is over, the writing will be on the wall, we'll have to admit it, that the women will have good and truly gone their separate ways, leaving us to a long and lonely breakfast for our consideration, including the grinding of the coffee

beans, the filling of the Britta pitcher, the watching
of it filtering, the buttering of both sides of a piece
of toast, the throwing of it away, the reconsidering,
the taking of the toast out of the garbage, the
opening of the back door, the tossing of the toast
onto the snow in the backyard for the squirrels,
the watching of the squirrels for several minutes,
the watching of the birds, the making of the coffee,
the drinking of the several cups at the kitchen
table, the becoming temporarily paralyzed with a
fleeting though nearly overpowering desire to
hightail it to the Chevron for a pack of cigarettes
(such laudable behavior deserving reward, the
marriage counselor might say), the resisting of the
many maddening moments to rummage through
all the stuff left behind (resistance, too, possibly
earning us an exceptional mark for behavior in the
exceptional behavior book), the rifling through
the unanswered questions, the empty bra in the
closet dangling on the rod like a filleted pike, the
women's summer clothes all gone, the difference

between the words *departing* and *going*, *going* and
departing, which is, one of us suggests, resolvable
by the Spanish word *vamos*, a word that graduates
the shade of that meaning between going and
departing, but then we should take a look here out
the conference room window, someone says, right
across the parking lot at that Payless Shoe Source
sign, perfectly intelligible despite the snow because
the sign is written in English, planted in good old
American soil, and now ask ourselves here, as
we're reading that sign, we need to ask ourselves
what country this is, leaving us a little bewildered
(from all of this, just *thinking* about it), a little
numbed out, so that it's already starting to sound
a lot like breakfast around here, where we're
already missing our wives, where, evidently,
everything's already desire, at least according to
what we've read in the women's literature, how
the *Upanishads* deems our desire as the fundamental
problem, how our actions are dictated by the
pursuit of our desires, so that what pathologically

optimistic and bright flight attendants over Amersfoort at this moment must desire is to make a fully orchestrated pass up their assigned aisles, because this pass is their absolute function, what they have been preparing for since their ascent into the airspace somewhere above the Netherlands, citrusy scents wafting from their rear-ends as they dole out thin pillows from overhead compartments, drape thin blankets over cold shoulders and exposed, bare thighs while darting fore and aft for last requests — if one desires water, a flight attendant will eventually appear, carrying a plastic cup of water — and it's because so many passengers are in want of so many things that the cabin of KLM Flight 4103 is absolutely humming with competing desires, all of it expressed in garish ambient lighting, the brightly scented flight attendants themselves unable to function otherwise (indeed, if they functioned otherwise, they would be captain, passenger or ground crew), as they dispense tomato and orange juices and rich, amber-colored cocktails to those who are despondent, to those whose prospect of divorce creates sorrow, whose attachment is creating longing, whose loved ones remain concerned for their well-being, no matter the circumstances of their suffering, their (the travelers') tears not shed over said despondency or suffering but because of conjunctivitis, so that they must recline their seat from the fully upright and locked position, and lift their faces to the ceiling of the cabin before applying the medicinal drops, and that, once the drops are applied, they will clearly see that coffee and tea service is now being terminated, that, in short, nothing lasts forever and everything has its place here (we remember how the women's literature locates this place in the mind, how, for example, we are apparently within all, and we are outside all, and when the great bedazzled, spandexed sage sees that the great Unity and her Self has become all beings, delusion and sorrow can never be near her,

for example, or something like this), and that after
the flight attendants stow and secure their metal
trundles in their proper places, they, too, can
settle into their seats for the long, overnight leg
between Amsterdam and Mumbai, a previously
unfathomable distance from here to India that
we've determined is 8,000 nautical miles, more or
less, the distance nonetheless that the women's
bodies will be forced to hurtle through if they
leave us, leaving us with only the memories of
those bodies, our memories themselves defined as
unmodified recollections of words and experiences
(Patanjali), which is undoubtedly the case, as
here's some fragment of a wholly irretrievable
memory of late summer that someone offers up,
about as vivid as the weather forecast for a
uneventful Wednesday late last year (smelling
vaguely of cotton sheets and Vic's Mentholated
Vapors, and sounding, vaguely, like a summer
cold), and some images of the fall just lived,
likewise an insubstantial montage of moments

without any ordering by importance — a shoeless child crying sop-footed in the street, a sneaker stuck in the grate of a sewer drain, four cold tater-tots on a white ketchup-smeared plate, the unmodified recollection of the word *tater-tot*, a figure in cool shadow standing across the yard in late March twilight, one hand on the back door knob, the other hanging earthward at the wrist, unoccupied — a montage best summed up by the old Austrian saying about nostalgia being the brain's Chlamydia, but a nostalgia nonetheless for those traversing nearly unimaginable distances, travels, in general, taking perseverance and good fortune in equal measure, as if the seat next to one of them is vacant, it's a miracle, and will soon be littered with fashion magazines, wads of tissue, cellophane bags of stale fruits and nuts purchased at an airport newsstand to keep the blood sugars elevated, a small plastic bottle of sulfacetamide sodium, a bottle of hand cream containing luxurious, light orange ribbons of peach-scented

hand cream to sooth their chapped hands, a tube
of beeswax to apply to their dry lips, and at thirty
thousand feet, at an airspeed of 450 knots, more
or less, they'll peer through the inky darkness,
down at an earth that faith alone insists is still
there, upon which lives are still being lived in
ordinary, more earthbound fashion, including our
own among the millions of husbands and wives
and children sleeping well on the ground, in direct
proportion to the sleep eluding the despondent in
the air, whereas, as a matter of fact (when we
come to think of it), we'll sleep *exceedingly* well,
unencumbered by the presence of our spouse's
body, our limbs allowed to stretch to the four
corners of a comfortable mattress, itself situated
in a simple, comfortable bedroom of a smallish,
comfortably modest house in the north-central
region of the United States of America, the safest
geographical landform in the entire world,
insulated from earthquake and invasion alike, but
on those rare occasions when we ourselves are

destined to sleep restlessly, skipping like a stone across the surface of erratic dreams in a sleep made shallow from drinking too much cheap merlot and eating too few canned raviolis, we will lie in bed perplexed and grieving, but tired, too (blame the wine or the grieving or the perplexity), and pick up our outdated copies of Fromme's *Visitor Guide to the Mysore Palace* (1963) or cross-referenced departure schedules — it's entirely possible that some of us are already preparing ourselves to follow our wives' contrails into the mystery of their silences to India, where we will demand their safe return — finally, and reluctantly, succumbing to the cliché that for every action there is a reaction, even though some more enlightened husband might therefore say bullshit, that if this is an illusion, then we shouldn't lift a finger to do a fucking thing, that the women may in fact secretly desire action, an action that accords with the activities of their minds, themselves moving very rapidly to their destination — where

they'll stop — so that we can already imagine
their return, their bodies on their home-bound
flight seeming to them to be still, an illusion in
itself, because the women's bodies will be hurled
through the sky back home to us at nearly the
speed of sound where, on that day of their return
(feels like a Sunday, for some reason) dusk will
finally come, and the balmy breeze that will have
been blowing all day will briefly shift from the
Southwest to true South (it will already be
springtime), pushing with it the traffic noise from
the bypass ringing the city, and then it will die
down all together, causing windows to be thrown
open up and down the block, the force of the
transition demanding a silent observation, and for
several hours, little will stir, until a small army of
airport shuttles arrive, silently coasting down our
streets, stopping in front of our various houses,
the abandoned inhabitants inside them having lain
down for a much deserved nap in the afternoon,
perhaps, and having apparently overslept, will be

sleeping still in front of a whirring box fan fixed in the open window, until we feel a hand wordlessly touching our heads, causing us to draw up in alarm, so that, in this way, we'll be reawakened.

THE END

Afterword from The Publisher

Contemporary publishing suffers under the unfortunate notion that creative writing (language as art) exists as a *product* to be sold rather than an *idea* to be explored, sometimes repeatedly, to fully understand whatever question or hypothesis first attracted the writer to the ideological territory.

Recall that Montaigne considered his essays (*essais*, literally, *attempts*) as parts of a whole that might never be achieved in one's lifetime. Trying, then — often from many different perspectives, in the same way Gertrude Stein would later write her cubist works — became critical to the development of the idea and the human. "I am myself the matter of my book," said Montaigne. The same is true for any writer, whether of nonfiction, fiction, poetry or hybrid.

Jaded Ibis Press elected to publish Christopher Grimes' novel, *The Pornographers*, and his short story collection, *Pornographies*. They are different versions of the same thematic exploration, which is exactly why we published both. Once you and I step outside the tiresome view that books are ultimately consumer goods and must be fixed at some point of "perfection" or else "fail", we rise to a goal much higher than what literature has, sadly, become: We seek to improve the individual, the culture, the society and the species by attempting to understand, through language, the whole as shaped by its parts – much healthier, less corrupt ambition.

I founded Jaded Ibis Press as a necessary "playspace" wherein writers could expand ontological concerns in a way that provides individual and cultural growth; that is, a way to become better humans. Because I am educated in and a practitioner of both creative writing and visual art, my view of what literature might and should be differs from the mainstream and, in most cases, the academy. I do not view a story as a final product but rather one part of a whole that shall only be complete when I die or am otherwise unable or unwilling to intellectually and creatively grow. For example, when exploring the ideas surrounding theoretical physics as it manifests in 2D visuals, I did not create one drawing and then move on to the next topic of exploration. Rather, I created 360 drawings, paintings and mixed media images, stopping only when I felt I'd gained sufficient clarity on a subject that had heretofore compelled me. This method of repeated investigation was a fundamental part of my visual art education; we drew, painted, sculpted and wrote about the same one object for an entire semester or year. The tremendous understanding I gained from the experience continues to inform my professional decisions.

Every book written is an attempt, regardless of what the publishing, marketing and book review industries claim. Knowing and comprehending this fact significantly adds to a reader's intellectual and aesthetic development, for rather than shutting doors before opening another, the reader constructs pathways through a vast and continually expanding library of related information and subsequent processing.

By publishing both versions of Grimes' narrative, Jaded Ibis Press provides readers with a more accurate glimpse into the writer's mind, the human mind, in general, and the history of and future possibilities for human language. We're tremendously excited to have had the opportunity to participate in this project.

Debra Di Blasi
Publisher-in-Chief
Jaded Ibis Press
Seattle, Washington USA

ABOUT THE AUTHOR

Christopher Grimes is the author of *Public Works: Short Fiction and a Novella*. His stories have appeared in *Western Humanities Review*, *Beloit Fiction Journal*, *Reed*, *Cream City Review*, *First Intensity*, *KNOCK*, and elsewhere. He teaches literature and fiction writing at the University of Illinois at Chicago.

The Pornographers is available in
four beautiful editions:

❖ full color with art by artist Scott Zieher ❖

❖ black and white ❖

❖ ebook ❖

❖ fine art limited edition ❖

for more information visit our website

jadedibisproductions.com